The Mark of Gleneil

The Mark of Gleneil

by

Michael Brander

The Gleneil Press

First published in Great Britain in 1998 by The Gleneil Press
Whittingehame, East Lothian, EH41 4QA
O Michael Brander 1998
The right of Michael Brander to be asserted as
author of this work has been identified by him in
accordance with the Copyright Design and Patent Act 1988

British Library Cataloguing in-Publication Data

A CIP catalogue record for this book is
available from the British Library

ISBN 0 9525330 8 1

Printed and bound in Great Britain by
Caledonian International Book Manufacturing Ltd

Contents

Preface

When the old unrestored west wing of Gleneil Castle collapsed in 1879 Professor Angus Alexander Neil, younger brother of the Clan Chief, went with it At work in the Muniments room on the Clan records he died a historian's death in a cloud of dust and dry rot. His body somewhat the worse for wear like many of his heroic forebears was buried in the family graveyard beyond the castle with his quill pen still firmly grasped in his hand, For many years the Gleneil historical records, which he was known to have been in the process of collating, were thought to have been destroyed at the same time. Surprisingly, however, in the 1930's, when the ruins were being painstakingly removed stone by stone for transhipment to the USA, three brassbound chests were discovered intact in the cellars, each filled with manuscripts of varying ages mostly in remarkably good condition.

It had long been known that amongst other inherited characteristics the Chiefs of the Clan Gleneil were inveterate chroniclers of their day, but from a hasty examination of the contents of the chests it was thought that these were little more than jottings of the 19th-century Gleneils. Pre-occupied as he then was with the abrupt and disastrous decline in the family fortunes caused by the 1929 slump the Chief paid little attention to the discovery. The chests were placed in the care of the family lawyer in Inverness, himself a Clan member, and there they remained, ignored and all but forgotten until the death of the last Gleneil of Gleneil in the direct line in 1949.

When the chests were finally examined, it was discovered that they contained an almost complete history of the Clan from the earliest days. Professor Angus Alexander Neil, a historian of some note (his publications include: *The Clan Gleneil in the '45; Montrose and Gleneil: A Monograph* and *A History of Highland Dress*) had been in the process of collating the documents, which provided a fascinating treasure trove of Clan material. It transpired that in almost every generation one or another leading Clan member, usually the Chief himself, had been a confirmed diarist. The result was an almost complete history of the Clan through each generation since its inception.

With the Clan Chief dead, a Committee of Clansmen was formed to decide how best to deal with the Clan papers. The Committee, however, as is often the way with Committees did very little. Throughout the 1960's and 70's little was accomplished. In the 1980's the services of Clan member Michael Brander, an experienced historian and author, were obtained and since then an editorial team has been hard at work.

Although the earliest papers were, naturally enough, amongst those in the worst condition it was felt desirable to start with them if at all possible in order to set out the historical origins of the Clan chronologically. The old sheepskin documents in a mixture of dog Latin, Norman French and even Gaelic, with occasional large gaps, caused by age and general wear and tear, posed some massive problems. With the assistance of numerous experts and all the advantages of modern forensic methods, as well as a good deal of inspired guesswork, the early diaries were to a large extent success-fully deciphered. The general meaning and the tenor of the text has as far as possible been faithfully reproduced.

The following is the diary of the first Chief of the Clan Gleneil transcribed as nearly as possible in his own words. It starts, as he started, with what was obviously one of the most unforgettable incidents in his long and eventful life. which literally left its mark on him and his descendants: The Mark of Gleneil.

Introduction

They came for me at dawn. I remember waking to the sound of their voices approaching, for, in spite of everything, at some time during the long hours of the night I must have fallen asleep. The sour stink of stale urine and the feel of the dank walls against my almost naked body quickly brought me back to grim reality. Then the flickering light of their lamp casting weird shadows round the dungeon revealed them. They were three of Saladin's Nubian bodyguard, all specially picked men, six feet or more in height, with shoulders like the span of an ox. Each wore an unsheathed scimitar through the belt of his baggy breeks, above which, like me, they were naked. Their heavily muscled oiled torsos gleamed like metal in the lamplight.

"This infidel is little more than a child," grunted their leader contemptuously, using a heavy hammer to knock off the shackles which held me spread-eagled against the wall, chained by wrists and ankles alike.

"Yet he started the landslide in the Wadi Halifa which took five hundred or more of the Faithful into the arms of Allah and disabled as many more," growled one of his companions. "He deserves his fate and let us rejoice in it. May the jackals eat his bones."

"Ha. He prostrates himself in front of us," their leader chuckled, as my knees buckled and I fell forward onto the ground.

Tucking the hammer into his waistband he caught hold of my wrist and jerked me one-handed to my feet.

"Get up, little dog's spawn," he jeered. "You've not got far to walk. Then you'll never need to walk again."

I made no reply for I saw no need to let them know I spoke their language and, truth to tell, I had been stretched so long between those shackles I had no need to feign faintness. Nevertheless with the resilience of youth I could feel the blood coursing through my veins giving me fresh hope as I was held upright and regained my balance.

"Come, you two. Take the little infidel between you and I'll take the lamp," commanded the leader impatiently. "If he won't walk you can drag him along between you."

Each of them obediently took a grip on my upper arm and lifted me effortlessly between them, scarcely conscious of my weight. Outside the dungeon the air of the desert, laden as it was with the smell of camel dung and campfires, smelt sweet by comparison with that stinking interior. The stars were still clear against the steely sky, but a faint glimmering in the East indicated the first approach of dawn and in these parts it is not long from dawn to sunrise. It was only a short distance to the Castle gates where the guards were waiting to let us through a small postern, which they bolted and barred behind us,

Once in the open we moved at a fast pace, with my feet only touching the ground at intervals suspended inertly between my two guards. Though I hung limply between them I could feel my strength steadily returning. It was not long, however, before we halted abruptly.

"Here we are," grunted their leader impatiently. "And no sign of His Highness yet."

By then dawn was already appreciably lightening the sky and beside us I could see all too clearly the fate that was awaiting me. A cross of cedar wood freshly hewn and the fragrance permeating the air, stood at a point where the ground started to slope steeply down towards the plain of Acre. Below us the lights of numerous campfires glowed and flickered fitfully in ragged lines and already a stirring and murmuring could be heard as the Christian armies of the Third Crusade began to prepare for the dawn stand-to-arms. Behind us a similar low murmur like a giant hive of bees disturbed inside the towering Castle walls indicated that Saladin's army was likewise preparing itself, and the high notes of the Muezzin calling the faithful to prayer sounded as herald of the dawn.

"Ha. He faints at the sight of his fate," commented the leader scornfully, as I tripped on the rough ground when they set me roughly down.

Though I could see no possible chance of escape it struck me as no bad plan to encourage them to think me quite harmless and I drooped between the two guards still holding me as if I might indeed faint at any moment. Meanwhile the light was improving with every passing moment and I fancied I could even see the first faint glow of sunrise striving to rise and seal my fate.

Although I continued to feign faintness I could feel within me the mounting tingle of excitement I have always felt before any action. If my guards' vigilance should lapse for a second I determined to seize my chance, despite the odds. As the moments passed and their boredom increased I had little difficulty in drooping miserably between them, letting them support my full weight, but all the time I was inwardly alert for any mistake they might make.

Then came the sound of galloping hooves growing rapidly closer. Within a few moments a white Arab stallion reared to a halt in front of us and I saw the grey eyes and hooked nose of Haroun el Fahid, the young Saracen Caliph appointed by the court the day before to supervise my crucifixion. Little older than myself, it was clear enough that he did not greatly relish the business in hand.

"When the sun rises," he commanded abruptly. "Let him meet his fate as has been decreed."

Wheeling his horse down the slope he remained only a few yards away with his back turned to the proceedings, gazing down defiantly at the massed forces of the Crusaders' army lining up on the plain below facing the high castle walls of Acre. Several hundred yards behind us the Saracen trumpets sounded their outlandish wailing. From the serried ranks below came a sullen growl like the roar of a pack of lions at the familiar ritual about to take place in full view above them.

Within seconds it seemed to me the glow in the East burst into flame as the tip of the sun rose finally above the horizon and day burst full upon us as it does in those climes.

"Now then, you two," commanded the leader of the Nubian guard. "Hold him in position while I drive in the nails."

It was clear they were practised enough, for without a moment's hesitation they each seized a wrist in both hands and forcing my hands flat against the arms of the cross spread-eagled me so that I was on tiptoe, my feet barely touching the ground. Hardly was I in position. with the man on my left holding my hand from behind the cross spread flat against the beam and the man on my right facing me, than I felt a stinging pain as the executioner-in-chief thrust a sharp nail into the back of my left hand ready to drive it home through my palm and into the wood of the cross itself.

For that one brief unguarded moment his legs were apart and his weight on the nail piercing the back of my hand, while his other hand was drawn back with the hammer preparing to drive it home. All their attention was concentrated on the task in hand. My wrists were held by a powerful guard on each side with their leader about to hammer the first nail through my hand, but at least I saw the chance for one last defiant counter-blow.

"Spawn of a thousand pigs," I hissed, at the same instant kicking him with all my might between the legs.

At my words he hesitated for a fatal second before my ankle caught him with all my power behind it full in the groin. As he doubled forward in agony the hammer blow came down hard on the wrist of the guard holding my hand flat against the wood. I heard the bone crack and his grip loosened instantly, their gasps of pain sounding as one. Tearing my arm from his weakened hold I felt the nail fly free as I reached for the hilt of the chief executioner's scimitar now protruding invitingly towards me as he bent forward hugging his groin. Despite the pain I felt in my hand I wrenched the weapon out of his waistband and swung it forward with all the strength I possessed at the exposed neck of the guard with his back towards me still holding my right hand. The heavy blade sharpened to a razor's edge sliced through muscle, bone and gristle effortlessly, severing the vertebrae cleanly so that one second his head was on his shoulders and the next it was a black ball spouting gore and bowling down the slope between the legs of the snorting stallion.

"Here's one for Gleneil!" I found myself shouting insanely.

Then switching the scimitar to my unhurt right hand now free again, although I have always been as good with the one as the other, I swung a blow at the back of the chief executioner's head still bent forward invitingly. In the instant a second black ball spouting gore was rolling under the hooves of the now frantically rearing stallion and I could not avoid feeling a fleeting moment's admiration for the balance and keenness of these Saracen weapons. Pausing only for a quick slash at the face of the remaining Nubian guard and seeing him fall back, I took three running strides and leaped on the back of the plunging stallion, which the young Caliph Haroun el Fahid was trying to control. Before he even knew what was happening my left arm was round his body binding his arms to his sides and I was as firmly seated behind him as a mating toad.

"Now ride for your life, or I cut your throat," I cried in his own language, clapping my heels vigorously into the stallion's flanks and slapping its hindquarters with the flat of the bloody scimitar.

With a mighty plunge the stallion shot forward towards the Christian lines as if propelled by a thunderbolt and neither of us could have stopped him even had we tried. It was only the mighty trenches, dug by the besieging Crusaders' army on the plain before the walls of Acre, that halted his headlong gallop by which time we were amongst friends. Thus it was that I acquired the mark of the nail on the back of my left hand which I bear to this day and which is also to be found as a birthmark on the left hand of my sons and of their sons also. It is a mark of which they and I may be justly proud for it signifies the founding of the fortunes of the Clan Gleneil.

On my triumphant arrival in the Christian camp I was knighted on the spot by the King, my father, himself. The ransom I later obtained from Haroun el Fahid was more than twice his weight in gold and precious jewels. My shield proudly bears the sign of the cross with a black head couchant on either side and a rising sun above it, with the defiant motto 'Cross me who dares!' Now, as an old man I am persuaded that it is perhaps time I passed on the full story of my life to those who bear, as I do, The Mark of Gleneil.

(Having transcribed this diary from a series of moth-eaten old sheepskins in very poor condition with not a few holes in them and from a script

written in a dog-Latin and Norman French with occasional lapses into Gaelic which at times made it almost incomprehensible as well as indecipherable, the reader must bear with the editorial team. We have tried to produce the essence of what was written and it has not always been easy. While undoubtedly a gallant, not to say impetuous, soldier of fortune the first Gleneil was unfortunately not well served by his early mentors. More probably he spent too much time with the huntsmen and men at arms and not enough in the schoolroom. All in all this is scarcely surprising. The first of the Gleneils, as well as being like many of his successors a compulsive diarist, appears at the same time to have been a remarkably freethinker, not bound by the mores of his day, a trait which he seems to have passed down the line to the majority of the Gleneil clan along with a markedly unusual degree of physical agility. Much of this may well have stemmed from him being a Royal bastard, a somewhat invidious position, where some tended to fawn upon him in the hope of favours, whereas others tended to take out on him what they saw as the iniquities of the social system. It may also have been because of this that he felt forced to excel amongst his companions. If the diaries seem at times surprisingly modern in tone allowances must be made for the difficulties of translation and also for the fact that Gleneil was very much his own man, clearly holding his own somewhat heretical views on many matters which in his day were regarded as completely accepted and unquestionable. Belief in such matters for instance as the Divine Right of Kings and the Code of Knightly Chivalry, to name only two of the sacred cows of his day, were amongst those on which he appears to have been a less than enthusiastic believer at times. On the other hand it may always be that he was in fact merely reflecting the true spirit of his day, and our own views have been somewhat conditioned by the novels of Sir Walter Scott and tales of the Court of King Arthur, which owe more to imagination than reality. It is evident from many of Iain Gleneil's comments that, while on the one hand they were able at times to make themselves a great deal more comfortable than one might have imagined, on the other life could be short and brutish and it was indeed necessary to be tough just to survive. In this respect his upbringing seems to have been ideal.)

Chapter 1

The Boarslayer

'Come here, Bastard,' 'Wait for me, Iain,' 'Where is the Bastard of Gleneil?' Such were the names to which I answered most frequently in my childhood, for in those days I was known simply as Iain, the Bastard of Gleneil. There was no shame in being a bastard of the Royal blood and I was always accorded the same rights and privileges as the sons of Fraser of Beaulieu, chief of the Clan Fraser, amongst whom I spent my childhood years. Sir Iain Glenoy, whose deeds of valour in the battlefield and in many famed jousting tournaments were legendary, was an honoured if distant kinsman of the Frasers and my cousin on the distaff side. This, coupled with the fact that I had been orphaned at birth, made me a special object of interest in the eyes of many of the more romantically susceptible females around Castle Beaulieu. Thus, to my contemporaries' envy, I could generally be sure of special treats from the cooks in the great kitchens at Beaulieu because of my particular birth and background. (*Despite lengthy research in the Records Office and the General Register House in Edinburgh and elsewhere we have been unable to find any trace of the name Glenoy, which may however have been due to to the condition of the sheepskin on which it was written. It is just possible, however, that Glenroy may have been intended. Even using ultra violet light and the latest forensic methods it has proved impossible to find the correct spelling. It has also to be admitted that Gleneil's writing and spelling are extremely hard to decipher at the best of times. Since he also occasionally used a form of personal shorthand known only to him the task of correct transcription of the original has at times been completely impracticable and the editorial team has simply been reduced to guesswork to fill in the gaps here and there.*)

The circumstances of both my conception and birth were admittedly unusual. I know to the day and hour when I was conceived. It was the evening of the 22nd of March in the year 1174, after a remarkable day of sunshine and blue skies, which had seen a morning and afternoon of brilliant jousting and feasting at Beaulieu, the stronghold on the Moray Firth of the northern branch of the Clan Fraser. At the splendid banquet that evening all eyes in the Great Hall were on the beautiful Lady Eleanor Glenoy, not least those of the monarch, King William the Lion of Scotland, who, it was said, could scarcely tear his gaze away from her.

"She has been the Queen of our Tourney this day and by God she shall be the Queen of our Bedchamber this night and ever more," he is reputed to have sworn according to the servants' gossip, which is often enough true in substance. It is certainly not disputed that, with the single-minded, even bull-headed, determination which characterised so many of his actions, the king rose before the feast was more than half finished and withdrew to his bedchamber taking the Lady Eleanor with him. The hour was close on seven. Soon after that I may confidently claim my origin. (*If his own records are anything to go by the back-stairs gossip at Beaulieu and at the royal court in Edinburgh was by far the most accurate source of information and the children of the nobility, including perhaps particularly the royal bastards, generally had immediate access to this invaluable source of news. All in all it is a considerable loss to history that by the nature of things, since servants were for the most part unable to read or write, their testimonies have not survived. For instance the serving wench in charge of the Royal Bedchamber probably had a much clearer idea of the exact line of royal succession than the Court historian, who was generally a hack employed long after the events to present the current monarchs in the best possible light, clean up any murky backgrounds or antecedents and generally thrust all the family skeletons firmly into whichever cupboards were conveniently available. It is this sort of thing that makes the honest historian and genealogist's life a nightmare. On the other hand in this instance, since the events of the day were likely to have been imprinted on the minds of the spectators, it is fair to assume that his statement regarding the date and time of his conception is accurate to the hour.*)

Unfortunately for both my mother and myself, news reached the Castle next morning that Henry II of England was facing a large scale revolt of his barons led by his eldest son, who was appealing to the Scots for help. Seeing his chance to regain the border land of Northumbria lost to the old enemy by his brother King Malcolm, the sovereign immediately gathered his retinue together and marched south. A month later he crossed the border with a hastily assembled army and began a siege of Berwick Castle. With most of his army dispersed looting the countryside and with no outposts set, a large English force appeared suddenly out of the mist while he was disporting himself, jousting under the castle walls, with a small company of his knights.

"Now will it be seen who is a true knight!" he cried characteristically, leading a charge against the vastly superior force of the enemy.

While such feats of knightly ardour and chivalry were no doubt greatly to be admired when perpetrated by romantically minded individuals, they were not behaviour suited to kings or army commanders. The rest is history. As was inevitable his horse was killed under him and he himself was captured. Led captive before Henry II, he was held in chains at the Castle of Falaise in Normandy and as part of the price of his release was forced to swear fealty to a king who had a total contempt for all the ideals of chivalry he held so dear.

He was only finally released from this shameful bond when Richard Coeur-de-Lion succeeded his father Henry II to the English throne in 1189. He willingly agreed to waive the oath of fealty in return for the sum of fifteen thousand merks to help towards a crusade in the Holy Land. Such is a brief summary of the events which explain my birth as a royal bastard. (*This was certainly not a bad bargain from the Scots' viewpoint. A silver merk was worth around thirteen and a half old pence, or slightly more than five and a half new pence, so that the total sum paid amounted only to something like £850. As Gleneil notes later, however, see below, it is more than probable that Richard intended in due course to repudiate the agreement at the first opportunity. It is rather regrettable that Gleneil seems to have had a somewhat cynical attitude towards his royal father's ideas on chivalry, although in the circumstances perhaps it was not altogether surprising in view of the fact that but for them he might well have been heir to the throne himself.*)

Yet, while I am thus fully aware of the day and almost the hour of my conception, I have never been sure within ten miles and forty eight hours as to where and when I was born. My mother, the Lady Eleanor, was returning to the Castle at Beaulieu in mid-November, accompanied only by a friar, an elderly tirewoman and a young wet nurse, in preparation for my birth, when they were overtaken by the great blizzard of 1174. This is still talked of over the winter firesides with awe and recalled by those who can still remember it as the worst in living memory, not so much for the severity of the storm itself, or the number of days it lasted, both of which were quite exceptional, as for the fact that it struck without warning in the middle of a day of bright sunshine. It thus took many unawares and caused great loss of life. (*While this does seem to have been an exceptional storm by any standards it is clear that the weather and its extremes was as much a general topic of conversation in Britain then as it is today.*)

Caught in the open, far out on open moorland, like many others in that fearful storm, my mother's small party forced their way on as best they could through the quickly gathering snowdrifts and the white inferno of falling snowflakes. It was not long before they realised they had lost their road completely. Eventually my mother and the friar decided, wisely enough as it must have seemed at the time, to halt in the shelter of a small copse of rowans and allow the storm to pass before trying to go any further. There they spent the interminable night sheltered to some degree from the full blast of the storm and with their horses providing some semblance of warmth. Some cakes, sweetmeats and similar dainty delicacies, intended as gifts for the young Frasers, provided them with nourishment of a sort for the evening, but it must still have been a miserable night with the wind howling and the blizzard raging as fiercely as ever.

With the arrival of dawn and the storm showing no signs of abating, they decided eventually after some anxious conclave to try to press forward while the horses were still capable of moving. For an hour or two they seemed to be making some progress, but the conditions were appalling and the strain on them all was considerable. Finally my young mother, exhausted by her efforts, felt the first pangs of childbirth approaching some weeks earlier than expected. There, somewhere in the wastes of Gleneil moor, with all the familiar landmarks blotted out by the driving snow and the countryside transformed into an unwelcoming white hell, in the pitiful shelter provided by the horses held by the friar, with only the assistance of her elderly tirewoman and the young wet nurse, I was delivered. Soon afterwards, with her end obviously approaching, my young mother was shriven by the friar.

"Let him be called Iain," she decreed, on being told of my birth, some time before she died from exposure and weakness. (*In the circumstances hypothermia and post-natal exhaustion, after the onset of a premature birth, quite apart from any other possible complications, would have been enough to cause her death. It is only remarkable that the child survived.*)

With my mother's death, the small party must have very quickly become aware of their own dire straits. Leaving her body decently composed behind them, soon to be covered by the thickly falling snow, but later no doubt to be torn apart by some of the ravening wolves in the area, for no trace of it was ever found, they struggled on together with the horses. (*At that time wolves were still one of the major pests in the Highlands of Scotland. They were hunted and killed as a matter of course and as late as the 17th century there was a bounty on the pelt of any wolf killed. In a Clan Gleneil Record Book of the 17th century cf. p.26 The Clan Gleneil History, it is stated: 'Any wolf seen to be reported and hunted instantly.'*)

The friar led the way on foot, for otherwise the horses would not face the storm. The tirewoman and the wet nurse came behind on horseback, taking it in turns to cradle me and keep me warm in their bosoms. Finally the prior started stumbling with weakness and suggested halting at ever more frequent intervals. It was obvious he was worn out with the effort of facing the storm and the horses too were showing every sign of exhaustion.

Apparently I bawled loudly for sustenance and was duly fed by my young wet nurse, although there was hardly any food left beyond a pouch of oatmeal to be shared between the three of them. The place the friar had chosen to halt was slightly sheltered from the full force of the blizzard and with the horses lying down they managed to obtain some sort of relief from the full force of the storm, which, if anything, seemed to have increased in fury. Thus the second night passed with them all huddling together for warmth and doing their best to protect me from the elements. In the morning the tirewoman and the wet nurse discovered the friar and two of the horses had frozen to death during the night.

The two women were then faced with the problem of whether to move on or stay where they were. Being countrywomen of courage, they decided to journey on, even though there was no sign of the storm lessening. Leaving the snow covered mounds of the dead man and beasts behind them, they forced their way onwards, taking it in turns to lead the two remaining horses. Somewhere around midday on that third day of the great storm the tirewoman collapsed under the strain. The young wet nurse stayed with her in the shelter of the horses which showed no desire to move any further amid the deep snow drifts.

At some time during that third seeming interminable night the tirewoman died and in the morning the young wet nurse found herself alone with only my infant self for company. Though young and healthy, after such an ordeal she must have felt close to exhaustion and despair. She sustained herself with the last pitiful remains of the oatmeal soaked in blood drawn from the more exhausted looking of the two remaining horses, after the manner of the clansmen with their cattle during the long and dark winter months. Then wrapping me firmly in her shawl and tying it closely to her bosom, she grasped the other horse by the tail and flogged it with the reins until finally it moved forward reluctantly into the storm once more. For several hours apparently, or so it seemed to her, she forced it onwards unmercifully until finally it foundered in a drift.

She, herself, by this time was close to complete exhaustion, buxom country wench that she was. It was only my crying which forced her to her feet once more and kept her staggering onwards through the snow. Eventually even her youthful stamina began to give way and she lost all track of time. How long she struggled on before her strength finally gave way it is impossible to say.

It was apparently the sound of my crying, feeble though it must have been, which came to the ears of two of Fraser's men busy fetching peat from a stack close to the castle walls during a temporary lull in the storm. By then the lass was in the last stages of exhaustion and, close to safety as she was, it is doubtful if she could have risen again. Soon, however, we were both inside the warmth and safety of the Great Hall at Beaulieu Castle. There, once fed with some warm broth, she rallied well enough to tell her story. With the vitality which characterised her throughout her long life, she then insisted on feeding me once more before falling into an exhausted slumber. Then, as always, for Jeannie Macdonald, my needs came first.

"So this is William's bastard is it? Well, if he's come through Gleneil in this storm he'd better stay," said Fraser, when I was taken up to the head of the table for him to look over as he dined. "If Eleanor wanted him to be called Iain, so be it. Let him be known as Iain, the Bastard of Gleneil."

Well pleased with his jest, he returned to his meat and I was thus casually accepted onto the strength of Beaulieu's inmates, as one more mouth to feed and one more brat running wild around the precincts of the castle. In practice I was fortunate, for, despite my lack of parents, I had a happy childhood. Treated mostly as just another of the numerous young about the place, I never felt the want of affection, nor do I recall being ill-treated. Life was rough and ready, maybe, but we all accepted good and bad times as we accepted the change of the seasons as just a part of life.

For me, at any rate, there was always Jeannie Macdonald to fall back on in times of trouble. My preserver and stout champion, by demonstrating a marked ability as a needlewoman after I was weaned,, remained on the castle strength as one of Lady Fraser's numerous attendants. Yet, though I was the kernel of her being, the very reason I suspect for her existence, she never spoiled me, for that was not her way. Whenever help was needed that she could provide, however, such as liniment for a twisted ankle, a bandage for a cut hand, or similar small comforts, I could rely on her. Just the knowledge that she was there when in need and always ready to be of assistance was an immense comfort to me in my childhood, even if I did not appreciate it as fully as perhaps I should have done.

Amongst the clansmen and women of every occupation who lived in and around the castle at Beaulieu, my two other favourites were undoubtedly Dougal Macloy, who was the chief armourer and man-at-arms, and Alistair Macgruer, who was the chief huntsman. Unfortunately they were barely on speaking terms with each other, which was a source of grief to me and of some amusement to almost everyone else. The origin of their quarrel was something of a mystery, but, although they were both confirmed bachelors, it was generally believed they had fallen out over a woman.

As befitted an ex-man-at-arms, Dougal was built like a square chunk of muscle and sinew, gnarled and thickset, his face scarred and riven from temple to throat on one side where he had been struck by a scimitar in battle against the Saracens during the Second Crusade. His proudest claim was that he had once been right hand man to my grandfather, Sir Iain Macloy, being now, as he put it, relegated to polishing the weapons and armour in the armoury at Beaulieu. It was, of course, a very responsible position and one he filled extremely well for there was little anyone could teach him about the weapons of war. He must have spent many happy hours passing on information to me on swords, spears, long-bows and cross-bows, of which he disapproved strongly, and showing me all the multifarious points of arms and armour and the well oiled belts that held the pieces together. While we sat all the while burnishing the coats of mail so that they shone as brightly as silver, now and then he would spring to his feet to demonstrate the correct way to use a falchion in close combat, or some other special piece of swordplay that his endless tales of battle brought to mind. (*It should be appreciated that in these early days the various pieces of armour were held together by a series of leather belts, or laces, holding them in place. This allowed them to overlap rather like a series of flaps. The knight was thus, as it were laced into the suit, by his squire or whoever was helping him put it on. Each smith, of course, had his own theories about how a suit should be fitted and the experienced could tell just where a suit of armour had been made and probably by whom, just as many people can tell each different make of car at a glance.)*

Alistair Macgruer was a very different sort of man, slim, fleet of foot and quick of movement. Lean and lithe, moving like quicksilver with his hounds around him, he was hard to follow when in pursuit of deer, boar, or other lesser quarry with his bow and spear. His face too was lean, weathered brown and hooknosed with a pair of steady grey eyes, hooded like a falcon's and almost as keen-sighted. He was an everlasting source of information on breeding, training and controlling hounds and every aspect of the hunt. When it came to knowing the ways of the wild I never met his like. He could tell, seemingly with only a glance at its tracks, or fewmets (*i.e. the droppings or faeces*) the age and sex of any beast and whether it was a huntable quarry. (*Such knowledge was an essential part of a huntsman's lore well into the Middle Ages.*) Although he seldom rode on horseback he was a wonder at controlling a horse. Indeed he seemed to possess an extra sense with all animals as if he could converse with them in their own language and make them do whatever he wished. His knowledge of pit-falls, snares, nets and traps of all kinds for taking any sort of beast, bird or fish was unsurpassed.

He it was also who taught me about the stars. His understanding of the constellations was in part self-taught and in part handed down by others. Apart from the ability to make one's way by land at night, as the shipmaster steers his ship on the sea, he was able to use the stars as a calendar. Taking two fixed points such as a tree and a mountain peak he could calculate the passing of the weeks and months. Thus when a mare was put to a stallion he would know to the day when she was due to foal and the same with many other animals. I found his lessons fascinating and it was a grounding I have found useful all my life. (*This innate understanding of the stars has been a part of country life over the centuries and is not related solely to navigation or finding the way at night, but also as a calendar relating to the gestation period of animals such as horses as Gleneil noted, but also, in particular, cattle and sheep. Sheep were not kept in the Highlands until the late 18th century because of the number of wolves, as noted above, but the sheep fanks, or stone circles, sited all over Scotland, into which the sheep were herded prior to being introduced to the Tups, or rams, were all sited so that a star, such as Sirius, could be seen above a prominent local landmark. The shepherd might be illiterate, but he knew that when that star appeared again above that point it was time to bring in the sheep from the hill for lambing. In the same way our ancestors could generally tell the time of day very accurately by the angle of the sun.)*

Another of his duties and delights was supervising the hawks in their mews, catching the young birds in the wild and training them to the lure, then entering them to game, the grouse on the moors and wildfowl in season. It was with him in the winter months that I spent many a dawn and dusk after the countless geese which annually descended on the estuaries, stalking and netting them or sometimes shooting them with bow and arrow. It was cold and often muddy work, but I have always relished the wild sound of the skeins of geese heralding the return of winter. Among my favourite pastimes, along with many of the young Frasers, was stalking and shooting or netting the hordes of wildfowl, geese of all kinds, mallard, eider and other ducks, which haunted the lochs and estuaries round Beaulieu in winter, the feathers and down of which were in great demand for winter bedding. (*This sounds like a very sporting as well as wide-ranging upbringing and many a present day wildfowler, or naturalist, would envy a time when the countryside must have been teeming with vast skeins of wildfowl. No doubt, however Beaulieu was exceptionally well placed in this respect. Although the majority of these birds were probably caught in nets it seems the 'art of shooting flying' with bow and arrow was also practised. Apart from using carefully chosen feathers as flights for arrows, as he noted the bulk of the feathers and down were used to stuff the mattresses and pillows of the senior Clan members. With coverlets of fur and skins of deer and other quarry on the floors, as well as roaring log fires, life may not have been as comfortless inside the confines of the castles as it may appear to visitors to the windblown ruins today.*)

Alistair was almost certainly a close relation, some said half-brother on the wrong side of the blanket, to the Chief. He had the advantage that as they had been brought up together as boys he had been taught to read and write. He it was who taught me the importance of recording the events and happenings of each day while they were fresh in the mind. By so doing, as he pointed out, it was possible to look back and compare different years and see how the seasons had changed and how this had affected the game and the hunting. (*Here apparently is the clue as to why Gleneil was to become a compulsive diarist, It all seems to have stemmed from the keeping of a game book by one of his boyhood heroes. It was it would appear the influence of the huntsman rather than his tutor we have to thank for this remarkable record. It all goes to show the importance of training the mind young, as the Roman Catholic Church have known for centuries. This, however, is a particularly interesting case since not only did Gleneil become a compulsive diarist, but he passed the trait down the centuries.*)

It was, however, from Dougal that I learned the art of archery, both with the long-bow and the cross-bow, as well as a rare grounding in swordplay which has been of value to me throughout my life. I also learned the practice and theory of combat with the battle-axe, the mace and the morning-star, the dangerous spiked ball on a chain used mainly when dismounted, which when well-aimed and powerfully delivered could crack a metal helm like an eggshell. I can still remember with what awe I used to peer at the serried rows of weapons of war, ranging from the great pikes with their gleaming sharpened heads, used by the foot soldiers to form a schiltron, or hedgehog, to repel the attacks of heavily armoured knights, down to the lines of two-handed swords, sharpened and pointed, ready for battle, or the ranks of long-shafted Lochaber axes with their deadly razor-edged double-heads curving like crescent moons. The suits of armour themselves, finely burnished beneath their light coating of grease, with their wondrous inlays of copper, silver and gold, standing on their hangers as if ready to do battle on their own always fascinated me. I spent many hours haunting the armoury listening to Dougal's monologues, while he instructed me in the use of each weapon, demonstrating the movements as if I were of an age to use it myself.

"You're never too young to learn, lad," he would say emphatically.

"Or too old for that matter, either. Once you start thinking you know it all, that's when you want to look out, but if you remember all the little things I tell you, you won't go far wrong."

Then he would seize the nearest sword and make a mock parry as if to ward off an attack from me.

"Now, whenever you take an overhead cut on your blade remember that leaves you with a straight riposte to the chest, the stomach or the legs. Your opponent has made his attack and for the moment he's wide open, so when you see your chance make sure to take it," he would emphasise his point with a sweeping curve of the blade. "And if you've made the attack and been parried make sure you get back on guard again quick. See what I mean." (*He sounds just like many of those old retired sergeant-majors employed in public schools throughout the land to teach the young both physical training and the arts of war. There's nothing they like better than demonstrating the art of using a bayonet with all the gory details of how they used one themselves and saved the day at some long forgotten conflict. At the same time they are very good at teaching such skills as fencing, boxing and unarmed combat as well the knees-bends and press-ups of physical training. Come to think of it what else could one do with old soldiers of this kind, especially in the days when there was no requirement for doormen at large shops or hotels.*)

When not with Dougal I could usually be found with Alistair, either in the kennels, watching him attend to the needs of his beloved hounds, or in the stables supervising the management of the horses, or in the mews with the hawks, or, better still, out in the open, learning the ways of the wild on the hill or in the forests. (*This sounds rather like the sort of random upbringing which might have been acceptable at Gordonstoun in the days when Kurt Hahn, the pre-war founder, was headmaster. He used to arrange for each boy to follow his own inclinations locally, with for instance a local garage if a keen mechanic, or a local gamekeeper if a keen naturalist. The probability is that the life at Beaulieu was rather less inhibiting. After all in the 12th century there weren't all that many inhibitions anyway and public schools even of the Gordonstoun variety hadn't been invented. There are, of course, those who may argue that they should never have been invented*)

*anyway, but the inhibitions would have arisen just the same. That's
modern life for you.*)

"See yon patch beneath the old oak there, where a boar has
been rooting for acorns," he said, one day when we were a long
way from home. "Look how deep his hooves have sunk and see
the spread of his tushes where he has turned the soil. That is a
mighty beast, the Great Boar of Gleneil without a doubt, though
he's a long way from his usual haunts. It's as well we were not
here half an hour earlier, or we'd have had to climb these trees fast
to get out of his way."

The mighty animal known far and wide as the Great Boar, or
sometimes just the Beast, of Gleneil had terrorised the neighbour-
hood for years. Fortunately it was not often seen in the vicinity of
Beaulieu itself, but for fully thirty miles around Gleneil he was well
known and justly feared.

As cunning as he was strong, he was notorious for his unpredict-
ability and, if even half the tales told about him were true, he was not
a beast to be taken lightly. He had been trapped a dozen times and
escaped on each occasion unscathed. He had been wounded on a
score or more occasions by spear and sword thrusts, by arrows and
cross-bow bolts, but never seemed to be seriously injured. Now,
scarred and savage, he was known to have killed at least half a dozen
armed men and severely wounded as many more again. His dislike of
humanity had grown so that whenever encountered he was likely to
charge immediately, regardless of whether it was a mounted knight
in armour or an old crone digging peat. It was reckoned fortunate
indeed that he seldom strayed far from his favourite haunts around
the Loch of Gleneil, where the marshy, boggy land and a tangled oak
forest close at hand provided him with an ideal and almost
impenetrable lair from which he only infrequently felt the need
to stir.

I must have been six or seven, certainly no more, on that outing
with Alistair, but I can remember being greatly struck not so much
by the sight of the great beast's tracks in the boggy ground, which
were impressive enough even to my uncomprehending gaze, as by
the gravity with which Alistair spoke. At that time I could scarcely

envisage anything which might force him to climb a tree. The thought of him running away from any beast was almost unbelievable and the Great Boar as a consequence somehow became confused in my mind with the colourful tapestry of a dragon hanging in the Great Hall at Beaulieu which had always impressed me. Thus I pictured the Beast as an animal with fiery nostrils and lashing tail, armoured scales and serpent's feet. In my mind he grew to be a monstrous beast indeed. (*The first European artist to portray a North American Bison purely from the description of various eye witnesses along with the help of his own imagination also produced an interesting result.*)

Perhaps one of the reasons I liked Alistair and Dougal so much and one of the few things they had in common, was that when demonstrating any point to me they each treated me as if I was fully grown and their equal . Thus, when we encountered those tracks, Alistair first showed me how to use a boar spear.

"Always make sure you bed the butt of your spear well into the ground," he said, digging the butt of his spear into the ground as he spoke to demonstrate the point. "If you can find a good tree stump, or a boulder, against which you can set it, so much the better. Wait for him to charge and see your point is aimed true for his chest, where his neck joins the ribs, if he raises his head enough. Then let him run his weight home to the cross-piece and after that hold on for your life, but if you've aimed true he'll kill himself by driving the blade deep into his heart."

As I held the great boar spear with its cross-piece some two and a half feet below the broad blade I tried to picture the boar frothing and bloody on the other end. It was then that the dragon on the tapestry came into my mind, so that thereafter I was never quite clear in my mind what the Beast looked like, although we had whole roast boar, with an orange thrust between its jaws served up often enough at banquets and I had frequently seen a sounder of striped piglets grubbing in the forest with their mother in attendance, or even an occasional good sized boar brought back from a hunt. All I really remembered clearly of his instructions was that the spear had to be thrust firmly into the ground, or against a tree and held there regardless or the dragon would win the day. It was a thought which seldom failed to send a shudder down my spine.

Apart from that one occasion, however, nothing more was seen or heard of the Beast of Gleneil in the vicinity of Beaulieu for several years. I myself developed into a sturdy ten year old, tousle headed and interested almost exclusively in the weapons of war and in horses, hounds and hunting. I was also, even at that age, a formidable archer adept with a bow, taught both by Dougal and Alistair, each in his own way an expert: the one on target shooting, teaching me each vulnerable point in the suits of armour, and the other on birds and the beasts of the chase.

I was, I fear, ever the despair of our elderly and somewhat ineffectual tutor, Father Middlemas, who supposedly taught us our letters and such schooling as was considered proper. I learned, willy nilly, to read and write and to speak Latin along with my fellows at an early age. As I grew older and stronger, however, the temptations presented by Alistair and Donald more often than not proved too strong to resist. I was never destined for a scholarly life. (*Anyone who has struggled to decipher his atrocious spelling and arbitrary choice of language would readily agree with this self-assessment. On the other hand let us give credit where it is due. It must have been partly the teaching of Father Middlemas combined with the example of Alistair Macgruer, the huntsman half-brother of the Chief, that resulted in Gleneil keeping the diaries on which this account is based.*)

At this stage I was little different from my fellows, except perhaps for a tendency to be in the forefront of any mischief. Whenever there was any trouble amongst the children it was often enough attributed to me, even when I was not involved. It is always useful to have a scapegoat on hand and I was chosen probably more often than was fair. My parentage, which had not seemed of much import one way or another in earlier days, about this time began to be a subject of discussion in the castle, and it was noticeable that in some eyes I could do no wrong. Jeannie Macdonald, who had always been my champion, soon set me to rights on the subject.

"There's some will butter ye up because you're yer father's son," she sniffed. "I'll say this for Alistair and Dougal, coarse though they may be, that'll hold no water with them. But just you watch your step with some I could name and never forget that your mother's family is as fine as any in the land."

My father, King William, had appeared to some to be disgraced as a result of his capture by Henry of England and his subsequent oath of fealty. Always a believer in the code of knightly chivalry, he himself regarded Henry's behaviour as unworthy and contemptible. He also saw the oath as extracted from him under duress and therefore not binding. On his return to Scotland, however, there were a series of rebellions fomented by discontented factions, mostly using this as an excuse for disloyalty, but by the time I was rising ten he had established himself firmly as undisputed king of Scotland once again. Thus it was that a number of people found it advisable to look kindly towards the royal bastard, whom they had previously ignored, or gone out of their way to abuse.

It was about this time that I first encountered James Macdonnel, the red-haired son of Macdonnel of Glengarry, neighbours of the Frasers to the south of Gleneil. Sent over to Beaulieu to gain experience in the tilting yard where Donald's training was famed throughout the Highlands, James was a few years older than the Fraser youngsters, who were mostly nearer my own age or younger. As a consequence he lorded it somewhat over us and we followed his lead without question, for at that age, of course, a few years makes a great deal of difference. It was noticeable that I was amongst his favourites and I, in turn, was amongst his most devoted followers. Although I might have noticed that both Dougal and Alistair showed signs of reserve whenever I quoted the sayings of my new hero this in no way diminished my regard for him. He had me totally under the spell of his charm and I could see no faults in him.

"James says the deer in Glengarry are better nourished than those around Beaulieu," I informed Alistair confidently. "That's why they all grow so much larger."

"James says all his father's armour has gold inlays," I told Dougal as he polished the silverwork on one of the finer breastplates in the armoury.

That neither of them replied to such comments with more than a comprehensive grunt, which in each case spoke volumes, I scarcely noticed. Whatever James told me at that stage was beyond criticism. Any words from his lips were treated as pearls of wisdom far beyond price and not to be questioned. I fear that I followed him around like a pet dog. Even Jeannie Macdonald's comments, scathing as they were, failed to affect my youthful hero worship.

"Are ye wanting to play follow-my-leader to a Macdonnel?" she demanded with typical forthright scorn. "And you with the finest blood in Scotland in your veins."

It was that Autumn, after an unusually hot dry Summer that the depredations of the Great Boar of Gleneil suddenly began to affect life at Beaulieu. With the ground in Gleneil, as at Beaulieu, dried to a tinder, it was thought some passing pedlar had carelessly set fire to the undergrowth surrounding the loch where the Beast habitually lay. A great conflagration had ensued lasting several days and lighting up the sky for miles around at night, in the course of which the Beast had lost his favourite haunts, for the whole place was turned into a desert of blackened cinders. Forced to forage further afield, the Great Boar had then moved northwards into Beaulieu territory and in a short space of time had begun to terrorise the area, for it was soon apparent that his temper, always mean and uncertain, had been in no way improved by this experience. It very quickly reached the stage where action had to be taken and Fraser himself decided to summon his followers to a great hunt, or Tainchel, with a view to settling accounts with the Beast for once and for all.

"The time has come to kill that brute," he decreed, as if it had never been attempted before. "And I will personally reward whoever deals the fatal blow with a purse of gold."

There was a good deal of excitement in Beaulieu at this pronouncement and also quite a lot of carping comment.

"I know fine who'll do all the work and take all the risks," grumbled one of Dougal's under-huntsmen. "And one of them with their fine suits of chain mail will spear the old devil and claim the gold."

"There'll be spears for all that want them, whether they've chain mail or no," snorted Dougal, overhearing this remark. "And there'll no doubt be huntsmen who'll take to the trees at the first sight of real danger, chain mail, or no chain mail."

Alistair who was also within hearing promptly made his displeasure plain.

"Anyone who weights himself down with chain mail when he's hunting a wild boar deserves to be gored," he said looking angrily at his luckless huntsman. "Only an overweight and over-age man-at-arms would think of doing so. If you hold your boar spear straight and firm no boar, even the Beast himself, can beat you. Any huntsman worthy of the name should know that well or he's not likely to stay long with me."

The huntsman, taking the hint, made himself scarce and Alistair and Dougal scowled at each other as was their custom during such exchanges before each going their separate ways. It was noticeable, however, that, with the announcement of the great hunt and the knowledge that shortly any able bodied male about the castle might very easily find himself facing the Great Boar, tempers grew shorter and quarrels tended to flare up over nothing. There was also a greater attendance at Sunday Mass that week than was customary except on ritual occasions. Father Middlemas was heard to remark cynically that the presence of the Beast was a great incentive to worship.

The day appointed for the great hunt came soon enough and all the Frasers and their clan followers in Beaulieu and for miles around had forgathered at their chief's command. Plans for the hunt had been made by the chief himself and his closer relations with the help of Alistair and Dougal when they had all met the previous evening. Those who required them had been equipped with suitable weapons by Dougal and there had been a good deal of heavy drinking and much loud joking and laughter, with everyone noticeably bright or gloomy according to their temperament.

Long before dawn the following morning, by the light of guttering torches, there was much less brightness and a great deal of short temper noticeable as well as a tendency to worried frowns, slight absent-mindedness and loss of appetite. Some, on the contrary, were full of forced brightness, making jokes and eating ferociously as if to deny there was anything the matter with them. There were others, however, who prepared themselves quietly as for any normal day with just a few practice cuts and thrusts to ensure that they were ready for action, No-one, however, was entirely unaffected for everyone knew the Boar's fearsome reputation. (*This sounds like the typical reactions even today amongst any group of men about to risk their lives in action. No doubt if Sir Walter Raleigh had crossed the Atlantic by then the majority of them would have been puffing away at cigarettes or pipes.*)

Eventually, not long after dawn, everyone had reached their appointed place and the sound of horns blown from various points of the compass indicated that the hunt had begun.

"I wouldn't mind winning that purse of gold," announced James brightly, smothering a yawn as we took up our position on the left flank. "But there's not much chance of the brute coming this way, more's the pity."

The plan of the hunt was comparatively simple. Alistair knew within a few hundred yards where the Beast had laired overnight and a heavily armed cordon of beaters was moving downwind towards the place carrying spears and burning faggots. It was hoped that on scenting the smoke the animal would head downwind to the chosen ground where the principal huntsmen of the clan lay armed in ambush waiting for him. In the centre, as befitted him, stood the chief himself, with his followers in order of seniority and strength on each side of him. As a youngster and son of a neighbouring chief, James was placed on one wing, with Alistair on one side of him and Dougal on the other. As usual I had attached myself to James, although officially I was too young and was not supposed to be there at all.

"Just you be ready to climb up yon tree, Iain, if he shows signs of coming this way," ordered Alistair when he saw me, pointing to a convenient easily climbed yew tree which stood close behind the pine tree where James was stationed.

Looking back on it all now with the benefit of hindsight and the knowledge I have since gained of such hunts, I can see, of course, that James has been placed so that even if the boar broke his way it was highly unlikely to come in his direction. Dougal, heavily armed, if slow moving, covered the lower ground some ten yards on the left, the most likely approach should the boar decide to come that way at all. Alistair, fast moving and well accustomed to hunting, was placed at the vantage point fifteen yards or so higher on the left, where he could see almost all that went on and keep a semblance of command as well as being on hand in the unlikely event of the boar breaking past Dougal.

On the face of it no ordinary beast would charge through the almost impenetrable tangle of wild brambles in front of us, leap a deep burn and then charge uphill towards us, when the most promising easy routes all lay downhill towards the centre of the ambush on our left. Of course, what had not been properly taken into account was that this was no ordinary boar. It had been hunted many times before and could be relied on to do anything but what was expected of it.

"Just hang onto my spear for a moment, Iain," said James airily, after the horns announcing the start of the hunt had been blowing for some minutes and various scattered yells had indicated sightings. "I've just got to empty my bladder. I shouldn't have had so much wine last night. I'll not be a moment."

"Thank you, James," I breathed in ecstasy,

Without thinking it in any way strange I seized the spear from him with pleasure, hardly able to believe my good fortune. My whole being was so attuned to the excitement of the hunt that the feel of the boar spear in my hands just then was a moment of pure joy, like the fulfilment of a dream. I was aware only of an overwhelming surging gratitude to James for the opportunity of letting me hold it for him. Hardly conscious of what I was doing I dug the pointed butt firmly into the ground at the base of the pine tree and knelt with both hands clasping the spear and sighting along the shaft at an imaginary boar.

"Il est hault! Il est hault!" cried the beaters, using the Norman French hunting cries then in common use.

"Tally-ho! Tally-ho!" came the echo from the treetops and the surrounding hills. (*The old Norman French hunting terms brought over with the Conquest by the Normans remain essentially the basis of hunting cries in Britain even today.*)

The sound of individual hounds giving tongue suddenly rose to a crescendo as the entire pack joined in full cry and swelled rapidly in volume to fever pitch. It seemed to be coming our way and I was staring eagerly to my front when the brambles started shaking wildly, then suddenly they bulged and burst open as a black humped shape appeared from the midst of them. It was the Great Boar himself and he bounded over the burn as if it barely existed. For a brief instant he halted in the open, switching his head quickly left and right and snorting at the air. Close behind him the black and tan of the foremost hounds baying frantically appeared in view.

"Il est hault!" I shrieked excitedly.

The shrill sound of my voice seemed to infuriate him. In an instant he was charging directly up the slope towards me so fast that I could see his body growing enormous along the shaft of the spear as I kept it aligned on his chest. His vast tushes gleamed white as his head switched from side to side even as he charged. His eyes gleamed a savage red, glaring defiantly and madly as he charged at the world which tormented him and refused to leave him in peace.

"Il est hault!" I heard Alistair cry from my left

"Il est hault!" came Donald's deep throated roar from my right.

I was conscious of them running towards me from each side and of the main body of the pack of hounds pouring in a black and tan torrent across the burn and up the hill; baying in full-blooded chorus, while the leaders ran, mute and determined, close behind the great beast and alongside him, striving for a hold. Regardless of all else, I concentrated on keeping my aim firmly on the great beast's chest as it loomed larger every second, so that I hardly felt it when the point entered the flesh until there was a sudden massive thud and a convulsive heave as his great weight hit the solid crossbar and the pointed butt slammed into the tree roots, burying itself a good six inches into the tree itself while the shaft continued bending and bucking like a plucked long bow.

For a fearful moment I thought the shaft was going to snap, but the stout seasoned yew wood held firm so that the monstrous beast was held at bay barely two yards from me. Squealing with fury, slavering and straining, pawing at the ground furiously in his efforts to get at me and tearing at the shaft with his great tushes, I doubt if I could have held him for more than a moment or two longer, despite the butt of the spear having been forced back so deeply into the roots of the pine, had not the leading hounds sprung at his throat and ears and sunk their jaws in his flesh. Shaking his head to rid himself of them and still trying to force his way against the crossbars towards me, he was a terrifying sight. I needed no encouragement to lean with all my puny strength and weight on the bucking shaft, doing my utmost of hold it firm against the roots.

"Il est mort!" bellowed Alistair, triumphantly from my left and I seemed to feel the blow as his spear struck home with all his weight behind it. It was a mortal stroke straight to the heart. Even so the great beast stubbornly struggled on, with his blood now flowing in great gouts from his head and nostrils as more and more hounds sank their jaws into his flanks and throat.

"Il est mort!" roared Dougal from my right, as his spear also was thrust home seconds later with all the force of his powerful frame.

At this final stroke a shudder ran through the great beast's body and his knees buckled slowly beneath him. Then, with something very like a human groan, he fell sideways. His legs jerked convulsively in his death throes, as he vanished under the main body of the pack of hounds swarming all over him.

As their triumphant baying rose to a new crescendo I rose shakily to my feet. I tried to brush a clot of blood from my face, for in his last moments the great boars's snorting breath had been spouting gouts of blood everywhere, but only succeeded in smearing it all over my cheek. For a moment or two I looked down at the great black mound of him barely visible beneath the hounds save for the bloodstained but still gleaming white tushes. Then, without warning, I suddenly found myself shaking all over and my teeth chattering beyond my control as I gazed at that fearsome mauled and bloody head.

"Are ye all right, lad?" asked Alistair anxiously.

"Aye, he's fine," replied Dougal, enfolding me in a powerful affectionate bear hug, so that I recovered myself in a minute. "And a credit to your training and mine, Alistair, old friend. Man, no quarrel's worth keeping up when we can share a moment like this one."

In that epic moment of reconciliation I was more interested in hearing the tenor of Alistair's reply than I was in his actual words and it was only later that I savoured them to the full.

"Aye, Dougal man, you're right," he agreed slowly. "And it's a proud man I am to be here with you. I think Gleneil has found a new master this day. Behold Iain, the Boarslayer, Master of Gleneil."

Chapter 2

The Arrival of the King

There is no doubt that the most painful moments of childhood are the betrayals, especially those involving the shattering of illusions. From the moment I had first met him I had idolised James Macdonnel of Glengarry as the epitome of everything graceful, brave and chivalrous. Though only a few years older than myself, he had from the first seemed to me a heroic figure. Now, as he appeared from behind the tree elaborately adjusting his doublet, his face was a little pale, but his smile as beguiling as ever. His manner was still the same easy mixture of condescension and bravado with which he had always treated me and all those he saw as his inferiors.

"Ah, well done Alistair and Dougal, I see you've accounted for the famous Beast at last," he cried. "I fear I was caught short. I thought those shellfish we had for supper last night were not fresh. A pity I missed the chance to make the kill, but who would have expected him to come this way."

"Aye! Oh aye!" replied Dougal heavily, in disbelieving tones, eyeing him dourly. "Caught short were ye, indeed? Up a tree, more likely, I'm thinking."

"It was Iain of Gleneil who slew the boar, with your spear," Alistair said accusingly. "I'm surprised you left a lad of his age alone like that, but he managed just fine. Better than many a good deal older than he might have done, had they been there and not up the nearest tree."

Under their accusing glares, James slowly turned a bright red and for once seemed strangely at a loss for words. It was then that I, springing to his defence in an effort to restore him to his pedestal, unwittingly completed his downfall.

"But James wouldn't . . ." I began hotly, then checked abruptly as I suddenly noticed the state of his hands, covered with tell-tale green stains from the lichen which grew thickly on the north face of the yew tree.

"James wouldn't . . ." I faltered again in strangled tones.

With my eyes fixed on those green stained hands I fell silent, filled with an inner sense of sadness as if I had lost something precious.

Both Dougal and Alistair had at once seen the giveaway signs and immediately reached the same conclusion I had belatedly drawn. They neither of them spoke and we all stood in accusing silence until James, by now crimson in the face, finally burst into a high pitched tirade of abuse, mainly directed at me.

"You always were a toad-eating, stinking little bastard, Iain!" he shouted, his voice suddenly shrill and high-pitched. "I am not going to stand here and be insulted by you or your lickspittle Fraser lackies. Churls will always find their like and their own level. Go your own by our lady way to hell and be done with the lot of you."

With this jumbled speech of defiance he strode off, still with the same easy grace I had always secretly envied. I felt an inward sense of sadness and desolation, but Alistair and Dougal watched him go in stony-faced silence. Then Dougal turned to me, his face serious.

"You have killed the Beast of Gleneil, Master," he said seriously, addressing me by the respectful title I had never merited before. "But you had better watch out for that young cub in future. He'll serve you a bad turn any time he can, if I know the kind he is."

"Aye, Master," agreed Alistair sombrely, following his lead. "You've made a bad enemy there, through no fault of your own. But meanwhile let's preserve your trophy head before the hounds have eaten it all."

I cannot recall what I said, if indeed I answered at all. While they set about the task of driving off the hounds from the recumbent boar my gaze was fixed on the retreating figure of James as he walked defiantly away, with that familiar graceful swagger in his walk. He had entered my life only a few short months before and now he was walking out of it as it seemed for ever. I felt as if a knife was turning in my heart, although another part of me wished that I might never see him again. I realised then that it is possible to admire and dislike the same person with an equal intensity at one and the same time. I also learned by bitter experience that grace and charm are not everything in life and may often conceal a mean heart and mind. I should have been grateful to James for teaching me that lesson so well so early in life. Had that been our last encounter I might indeed have been thankful to him in after years, but I was to repay the debt in full many times over, for our lives were to be strangely intertwined.

As Alistair blew the triumphant yet sad notes of the Mort over the corpse of the Beast of Gleneil I felt a prickle of tears behind my eyes, but they were for the passing of a friendship, not for the boar. I blinked them back and turned to Dougal, when he broke the brief silence as the last notes faded away in the upper air.

"You may live to be a hundred, Master," he said solemnly, continuing to address me with the title which still sounded strange to my ears. "But let this day stand in your mind, for today you proved your manhood in a feat few grown men would have cared to equal or stood as well."

"Aye, Master, this was a worthy beast indeed," marvelled Alistair. "See these tushes, over a foot in length and three or more inches round. I have never seen the like in all my years as a huntsman. This is a beast that has accounted for fifteen men and women as well as half a dozen men-at-arms and defied the spears of hundreds of hunters. Men have been knighted for lesser deeds."

At that moment I could still only taste the bitter ashes of a dead friendship and could feel little pride in the death of the Beast of Gleneil. However, as the rest of the hunt assembled and Alistair and Dougal repeated their story with embellishments I gradually began to recover myself. My Fraser contemporaries were duly envious, or awed, depending on their age and temperaments. Amongst the older clansmen and women there was nothing but relief, for the Beast of Gleneil, while not a frequent marauder, had been seen often enough recently to earn himself a general thanksgiving at his passing. There was also a widespread sense of relief, as they marvelled over the size of the Beast at close quarters, that they had not had to confront him themselves. Fraser of Beaulieu himself was lavish with his praise but even he could scarcely conceal a note of thankfulness after examining the corpse that he had not had to face the Beast in full charge.

"Well done, my boy," he cried. "You're a worthy sprig from the royal line. Your father would be as proud of you as I am. You shall have the purse of gold on our return to the Castle."

"No, I thank you, sire," I replied without thinking. "Let Alistair and Dougal share it together as they shared the Beast with me."

"Well said," replied Fraser, showing his teeth through his beard in a rare smile of approval. "So be it then. I see Alistair and Dougal are in the right and Gleneil has a new Master this day. Well at least we shall hang your trophy in the Great Hall to mark this day in the minds of all. Now as the victor you must lead the hunt back to Beaulieu."

There was great rejoicing at Beaulieu that evening after our triumphal return. The Great Boar of Gleneil was accorded the same fate as conquered Emperors and Generals in early Rome, being escorted back in triumph and laid out so that everyone could see him and rejoice at his downfall after his long reign of terror. In many ways he struck me as far more terrifying in death than he had in life, for then I had not had time to study him closely or to be greatly frightened. When I saw him laid out ceremoniously and could fully appreciate the great bulk of the beast, the sheer menace he still generated even lying dead in the Castle forecourt, I realised how lucky I had been.

"I don't know how I managed it, Alistair," I confessed, filled with wonderment at the muscle power that had been in him. "I just dug the butt of the spear in against the tree roots and held it steady as you said I should. He did the rest himself."

"Aye, Master," replied Alistair with the flicker of a smile. "But you did the right things and you didn't flinch when you saw him coming. You will kill many more boars in your lifetime, I am sure, but I doubt if you'll ever see his like again."

It was on the tip of my tongue to tell him to stop calling me 'Master,' but I knew that he would reply that while I remained un-knighted he could not truthfully call me 'Sire,' to which, of course, there was no answer. Following Alistair and Donald's example and encouraged by Fraser himself, the clansmen and women at Beaulieu thereafter always addressed me formally as Master, while my companions, of course, continued as before to call me Iain, the Bastard, or Gleneil, to which they now added Boarslayer by way of a compliment, when they felt so inclined.

There was one absentee from the triumphant rejoicing at Beaulieu and that was James Macdonnel, who, it appeared, had returned in haste to Glengarry. He left word that a messenger had arrived with an urgent summons for him to return home, but no-one ever admitted to seeing such a man arrive or depart. It was noticeable too that in all Beaulieu I was almost the only person who seemed sorry that he had gone; excepting possibly a simple-minded serving wench soon seen to be heavy with child, who attributed this to his attentions, although whether that was true was open to question, for as Alistair put it there were several who had ridden that willing mare.

As to the final disposal of the Beast of Gleneil, that proved more difficult than might have been anticipated. Having survived for an unknown number of years, he seemed to consist solely of gristly muscle and sinew, so that considered solely as a lump of several hundred weights of meat he was totally uneatable. Even the hounds that had torn at him unavailingly when he was alive were defeated by his flesh until it had been cooked for many hours in the vast cauldron in which their meat was prepared. His skull, with its gleaming great tushes, was eventually hung, as Fraser had decreed, in the place of honour over the great doorway of the main hall of the castle, where it remained for many years, the subject of numerous eyewitness accounts each varying as greatly from each other as from the facts.

(With no actual measurements given it is of course impossible to estimate the boar's size, but even allowing for exaggeration it must have been a quite outstanding beast. The mention of the tushes being 'over a foot in length and three or more inches round' would appear to make them quite exceptional as Alistair the huntsman indicated. There is however a mention by Boethius of a boar killed in Scotland around 1124 which had tushes of a similar length, described as having a diameter of 3 inches, so

that clearly there were some remarkably large boars to be found in Scotland around that period. Good tushes today might measure around 9 inches and given tushes of such exceptional length it is perhaps not unreasonable to estimate the beast as weighing somewhere around 600 lbs and measuring over three feet six inches at the shoulder and something over six feet in length. This would make it a very formidable animal by any standards and far larger than even the most outstanding beasts today. It was well-named the Great Boar of Gleneil.)

Truth to tell I had soon heard quite enough of the subject myself, but fortunately news of an impending royal visit to Inverness the following winter soon occupied everyone's mind. Questions such as who would be attending the court there and whether the king would come to Beaulieu quickly replaced the saga of the boarhunt as the principle topic of conversation. The entire castle was gripped with excitement at the prospect and rumours abounded, each wilder than the last. Then finally it was confirmed by Fraser himself; the king was coming and the date was fixed.

In many ways the news made matters worse. Everyone was seized with determination to show themselves at their best. The men-at-arms under Dougal trained harder than ever and burnished the weapons and armour daily. The huntsmen under Alistair marked the best hunting grounds and the likeliest beasts. The sewing women went to work on fresh gowns for the ladies and the ladies themselves were in a complete state of frenzy at the prospect of the royal visit. Amidst all this commotion, to my relief, the Beast of Gleneil was largely forgotten.

In some ways, however, the royal visit also posed its problems for me.

"You'll be looking forward to meeting your father at last, Iain, will ye not?" asked one old crone, with a malicious leer on her lips. "Ye've never met him yet, have ye?"

I was tempted to ask if she had any memories, or even knowledge of her own begetter, or indeed of those who had sired her various offspring, for she was as notorious for her loose morals as her loose tongue, but experience had taught me that it was always better to ignore such comments and turn a smiling face to the world. Jeannie

Macdonald had trained me well in that respect as in so many others over the years.

"It will certainly be interesting, Mistress," I agreed with a smile, continuing on my way without pausing, so as to allow her no further license.

That slatternly gossip was by no means the only one to raise the subject, however, so that before long I had almost begun to wish that the visit was over, or that something else would arise which would cause it to be cancelled yet again, such as another war with the old enemy south of the border. One part of me wished passionately to see my father and another part of my mind as passionately rejected any approach to a father who had never acknowledged me over the years. Jeannie Macdonald must have sensed something of my inner turmoil for she put it to me clearly enough.

"You'll maybe have thought your father might have sent for you before this," she said, with a penetrating look at my troubled countenance. "But you should mind that he's probably never even heard you exist all these years. It's not as if he's been near Inverness since you were born and Fraser himself has never been near the court."

As she no doubt intended this thought comforted me considerably, but then came the news I had hoped for earlier, that the royal visit was unlikely to take place because preparations were in progress for a Crusade to the Holy Land. This was followed by an announcement that the Crusade had been postponed for at least a year because the Pope had pronounced against it, and once again it appeared the royal visit was to take place after all. Twice more rumour said that the visit had been put off and twice more it was said it would take place as planned, with the dates changing every time. Finally, after everyone at Beaulieu had several times worked themselves up to a fever pitch of expectancy and then fallen into the depths of despair, the great day was suddenly definitely fixed and only a week away.

"The Fraser himself is wanting you," one of the men-at-arms informed me that evening as I returned, muddy and bedraggled from a day on the hill with Alistair noting the whereabouts of the best beasts for the royal hunt. "He's been asking for you for most of the day and he's not in the best of moods."

I made haste to make myself presentable, washing my head, arms and muddy legs in a tub of water and scrubbing myself dry as quickly as I could. Even so I was still somewhat bedraggled and more than a little apprehensive as I entered his presence in the Great Hall. It was seldom we boys were called before Fraser himself and usually only when we had offended in some way and were being hailed up for sentence and punishment. For once I had a fairly clear conscience, but I recalled uneasily snatching a loaf of bread fresh from the ovens that morning, before my old friend Mistress Fiona Sim in charge of the bakery could protest. I had fled with her shrill curses in my ears and I wondered uneasily if she had finally complained as she had often threatened to do to the Chief himself. I was busily thinking of excuses as I slipped into the hall.

"Ah, there you are at last, boy," he said, cheerfully enough, when he saw me. "I hear you've been out with Alistair. Well, I suppose that's no bad thing. I hope you saw some worthy beasts for the royal hunt? But we can't have you dressed in rags like that when your father comes, can we? Off you go to my lady and see what she want's done with you. I expect you'll find that she's ready for you. She's been pestering me about all you boys this past week or more."

Relieved that it was nothing worse, I took myself off thankfully. Most of my Fraser foster brothers and sisters had spent prolonged periods during the past weeks being drilled and dressed in preparation for the great day, complaining bitterly the while. By spending most of my time on the hills with Alistair, I thought I had escaped, but, of course, I might have known better. In fact it was Jeannie Macdonald I had to thank for this attention, as I soon discovered. I might have known that she would have seen to it that I was not forgotten, as I fondly thought had been the case.

My lady, the chieftain's wife, was normally an easy-tempered somewhat indolent and forgetful female, but it was clear when I went to her apartment that these were far from normal times. Seamstresses, under the control of Jeannie herself, serving maids, daughters and all those miscellaneous unmarried spinsters remotely connected with the family and many others I barely recognised, were milling about the apartments seemingly in a state of unending bustle and confusion. It reminded me of an anthill disturbed with a stick. This was just such a scene of orderly chaos.

"Ah, Iain, come here at once, boy," my lady's voice cut through the shrill buzz of muted female voices. "Where have you been all day? I've been asking for you everywhere. Now Jeannie, come over here and let me have your advice."

I saw at once why the man-at-arms had said the chief as not in the best of moods. It looked as if Beaulieu was in a state of siege. Certainly the womenfolk were up in arms and determined to present themselves and their menfolk at their best for the royal visit. Young though I was, I knew better than to argue. I went forward obediently, if reluctantly.

"It's all right, boy," she said in exasperated tones. "I'm not going to bite you."

In her mood at that moment I would certainly not have put it past her. She was in the grip of one of those female fits bordering on hysteria when everything is subordinated to one end. In the Spring, coinciding with the nesting frenzy of the birds around the castle, it generally takes the form of moving all the furniture to wash down the floors and polish the woodwork, then beat and clean the hangings and tapestries. Woe betide any male who objects or intrudes on these periodic fits. It is the same, more often than not, with wedding feasts and ceremonial banquets, after tourneys, tainchels, (*organised hunts, see above*) harvest festivals and similar celebrations. In female eyes the royal visit was clearly one of the more important occasions and merited all the effort they could expend in preparations to make it perfect.

(*The first Gleneil of course belonged to an age when sexist thoughts could be expressed freely and when feminist viewpoints were supposedly always kept suppressed. Just the same it is fairly clear from Gleneil's comments that even then women had their way when they wished to do so. The spring cleaning frenzy which he describes would appear to be one of those natural phenomena which occur in Nature in all species including Mankind.*)

As Jeannie Macdonald approached, I saw from the abstracted look in her eye that I could expect no help from her. I was subjected to ignominious twistings, turnings and proddings as she and my lady took my measurements. Then various cloths were set against my person and duly commented on, as if I myself were no longer present.

"Not that mauve damask, with his fair hair. Anyway there's not enough of it."

"Try this length of cloth of silver and see how it goes with this hose of green silk?"

I stood without complaint until finally they were satisfied with the results of their deliberations. Then her Ladyship was even prompted to say a kind word to me.

"There! That wasn't so bad, after all, was it, Iain?" she demanded. "Anyway, you've been a good lad and I trust your father will be proud of you. You favour your mother's side more than his, but you've more than a trace of your grandfather, Sir Iain Glenoy. He was a fine figure of a man and all the maidens vied for his favours at the tourneys when I was a girl. I remember we all thought him a very splendid knight . . ."

Her lips curved in a reminiscent smile and her voice faded for a moment as she recalled times long past. Then she recollected herself with a shake of the head and her brisk manner returned.

"Well, that's you dealt with, anyway," she went on. "Now be on your way and just make sure you do credit to the Frasers when your father comes to Beaulieu."

I slipped away with alacrity lest she changed her mind, or Jeannie produced another cloth to try and they then decided to set the seamstresses to work on some other choice. Fortuitously enough their attention was distracted at that moment by one of the serving girls spilling a pitcher of wine over a length of cloth. As I closed the door of the chamber I could hear a stream of invective of which any fishwife would have been proud being directed at the head of the unfortunate girl. For the rest of that seemingly protracted week, like most of the other males in Beaulieu, I did my best to occupy myself with matters throughout the day that would keep me well out of harm's way.

"I've been setting up pavilions for a tourney on the old tilting ground these past two days," grumbled Dougal. "Now she's talking about having them brought round to the front of the castle instead. It's enough to drive a man demented."

Even Alistair was unable to escape the general turmoil that surrounded the preparations.

"She seems to think I can produce enough venison for two days' feasting," he said in tones of disbelief. "And still provide his Majesty with a day or two's choice hunting as well. She's so full of preparations that there's no arguing with her, or getting her to see sense. Even Fraser himself cannot say a word to her."

There was no doubt that the chief himself was as careful as anyone not to interfere with his wife's preparations. Of course I realise now that she saw this as an unrepeatable golden opportunity to find suitable husbands for her brood of daughters and it was because of this that she had stirred herself from her usual state of happy indolence. Having made this point plain to her husband she had also ensured there would be no interference from him. With the entire castle and clan at her bidding for once, the whole affair had gone to her head like new wine. As the great day approached she scattered commands all around, quickly followed by counter-commands, like so many bolts from a cross-bow, with the result that confusion seemed to reign everywhere. Then, somehow or other, the week came to an end and suddenly as the great day dawned everything seemed to be more or less ready, or at least as ready as it was ever likely to be.

I remember dressing that morning in my new doublet of the silver cloth and mighty stiff stuff it was too, chafing my neck arms and wrists whenever I moved incautiously. The hose had twice been changed and a dark blue thick wool was the final choice. I daresay the result looked well enough, but it all felt extremely strange and scratchy. I suspect that almost everyone else wearing their new finery felt awkward and uncomfortable as well, but it was hard not to feel that all eyes were on you personally. Thus the small party of Fraser children, amongst which I was naturally included, standing by the castle entrance gates were all much more silent and self-conscious than usual with scarcely a word to say to each other for once.

"Here he comes," someone cried suddenly and we all craned our heads forward.

A mounted herald carrying the king's banner came forward at the head of the horseback procession. Behind him, side-by-side with the chief, clad in gorgeous cloth of gold, was a red-faced fierce-looking elderly man, as I thought, being then at an age when anyone over twenty seasons seems old. He must only, I suppose, have been then about thirty five, but the years of imprisonment may have aged him, and to a ten year old he seemed elderly. The thing that struck me most about him was his powerful beak of a nose and his bushy eyebrows above it, which gave him something of the look of an eagle.

"Hurrah," we cheered obediently, as we had been taught, and the girls curtseyed low, while the boys made their deepest bows.

He acknowledged our cheers and those of the clansmen and women lining the roadway with a smile and a cheerful wave of his hand, and this somehow made him seem more human to me. Then for a moment he seemed to be staring straight at me and suddenly he was reigning his horse to a standstill

"That's the lad you mentioned, we'll wager," he said to Fraser alongside him.

"Aye, sire," replied the chief, beckoning me forward. "Come, Iain, make yourself known to your father."

I stepped forward awkwardly, stiff in my new finery, and made my best bow. Then I turned my face up to gaze more closely at this magnificently dressed stranger who was apparently the king, my father, I had heard so much about.

"My God, he's like Eleanor. The same eyes and colouring," he said slowly, as we gazed at each other. "We'd have known him anywhere."

"He's your blood too, sire," Fraser reminded him. "He's made himself acknowledged as Master of Gleneil and earned the title of the Boarslayer. Wait till you see the tushes of the Beast. Over a foot long and more than three inches at the base! Not only that, he gave away the purse of gold I offered him as reward. Spurned it to my face like the blood royal."

"Ha," snorted my father, looking fiercely at me for a moment, before his face broke into a broad smile and he leaned forward to lift me one-handed onto his saddle bow. "Come Iain, Master of Gleneil and Boarslayer. Remember always that you are the son of the king. From now onwards we must get to know each other better."

With me in front of him astride the withers of his great grey war horse he rode on towards the castle entrance. Once there he set me down and swinging his leg over the crupper of his saddle joined me at the castle steps.

"Now," he cried. "Show us the head of this wonderful Beast of Gleneil of which we have heard even in our court in Edinburgh."

I hung back to make way for him, but he seized me by the hand and with Fraser beside us, led the way into the Castle and through to the Great Hall. There we stopped in the great doorway and he examined the trophy for a moment in silence.

"Odd's teeth, it's not possible," he cried. "No lad of barely eleven years could face and kill a giant boar of those dimensions."

"It's as true as I stand here, sire," replied Fraser stoutly.

For the moment my father seemed lost for words and turned his gaze searchingly upon me.

"I dug the butt of the spear well home against a tree stump," I explained earnestly, yet again. "And I caught him right through the main artery of the throat so Alistair said."

"Alistair is my huntsman, sire," explained Fraser, hastily. "The lad was not really meant to be part of the hunt, but he got hold of a spear. Both Alistair my huntsman and Dougal, my chief man-at-arms, were close by and were the first to go to his aid, though they both say he had him dead already."

"So! He gave the purse to them, did he?" nodded my father. "Of course! A touch of Eleanor there, don't you think?"

He turned his gaze to me again and his stern features were split by a broad smile, which creased up the corners of his eyes and made him seem much more human and friendly.

"You'll be accompanying us back to Edinburgh now, Iain," he decreed. "We must get to know our new found son, the Master of Gleneil and Boarslayer extraordinary."

He turned to the chief and exchanged a meaning look with him.

"Your lady was saying that she would be obliged if we would take one of your daughters as lady-in-waiting at our court," he said thoughtfully. "We have heard you have four of a suitable age who might be willing to accompany our son when he comes with us as a page. And it may be that one or more of your sons would be of an age to accompany him as pages also."

I was impressed to see the chief sink on one knee and bow his head in acknowledgement.

"Sire, I thank you, as will my lady also," he said. "She will be greatly honoured."

They were both smiling at me and at each other. I realised with a leaping heart that something very satisfactory had somehow been accomplished and that in part at least it seemed I was responsible. Not only had the visit started better than I had ever anticipated, but it also looked like ending well too.

The next week or so remain in my mind for ever as a blurred whirlwind of perpetual motion. My lady, once informed of the king's commands, became even more frenziedly active. The banquet that night was a memorable occasion, so I am told, for I went to sleep early in the evening. The hunt the next day was successful for my father killed a royal stag and a large boar, though somewhat smaller than the Beast of Gleneil. In the Tourney held a few days later he acquitted himself well. He was thus particularly pleased with both Alistair and Dougal and gave them a purseful of gold apiece on leaving,

All in all the visit proved a great success, and the Fraser sons and daughters accompanying me to join the court in Edinburgh left with the royal party in something of a daze. As the girls' seamstress, companion and guide, Jeannie Macdonald was also included; her part in my rescue being duly acknowledged. We then travelled seemingly endlessly. We first made a circuit of the various highland chiefs until we arrived at Stirling and from there journeyed on to Edinburgh, where we were informed we would meet the court at last. Quite what I had personally expected I do not know, but when we did at last arrive in the courtyard of the castle my eyes were almost closing with weariness. All I do know is that it was with a sense of deep foreboding that the first person I set eyes on as we crossed the drawbridge was none other than James Macdonnel.

I saw him staring full at me. As our eyes met he paled for an instant, then his lip curled in a bitter sneer and he turned away with a disdainful toss of his head, but not before I had caught the look of sheer malice in his gaze. With a shiver of premonition down my spine I recalled Donald's words. 'He'll serve you a bad turn any time he can.' and Dougal's sombre agreement;' Aye, you've made a bad enemy there.'

A moment later we were in the Castle courtyard and amid the hubbub and confusion of our arrival I soon forgot that first fleeting impression. The next hours and indeed the next days were a blur in my mind as I tried to fit into an entirely new way of life. There was little time at first to do anything but try to comprehend this new world in which I had suddenly found myself pitchforked headfirst.

(*William the Lyon was amongst the last Scottish kings to continue the custom of holding court around the country. Eventually even he appears to have given up the business of constantly journeying round the country and opted instead for staying put and holding court permanently in Edinburgh, the Capital.*)

Chapter 3

On the End of a Bell Rope

After a few days I began to find my feet in my new surroundings. I was put under the ostensible charge of one of the principal ladies-in-waiting, Lady Margaret de Brus, irreverently nick-named Auld Meg by all those nominally under her control. She mothered those pages under her rather like an old hen, although she could be stern enough when the need arose and there was a good deal more to her than at first met the eye. She also looked after some of the younger ladies-in-waiting, so that I still saw a lot of the Fraser girls who had come south with me.

Since we all felt new and strange we tended perhaps to form our own small clique, but in these surroundings that was natural enough and as we soon found out the entire court was composed of similar small groups each with their own interests in common, banding together with others when it suited them, or else in more or less permanent open enmity. There was little of that communal feeling, or of belonging to one large family that there had been at Beaulieu and at first it all felt very strange and unwelcoming. Too often, even as a youngster, it was necessary to curb one's tongue to avoid a sneer, or reprimand, from an opposing camp, and the perpetual feeling of intrigue and malice was unsettling to innocent newcomers.

I soon realised, however, that there was a whole largely separate world of grooms, huntsmen, men-at-arms, serving men and wenches, seamstresses, cooks and scullions, as at Beaulieu, who, on the whole, clan loyalties apart, cared little for the various groups lording it over them, and who formed their own separate world. As a young page, even of the royal blood, I was readily enough accepted into this inner world, which I found quite as fascinating as the other, with all the scandal and gossip instantly available and quite different interpretations put upon it. I thus contrived to have a foot on both sides of a clear divide and benefited greatly thereby, learning far more about human nature than I would have done had I been restricted to one side of the fence alone.

Beyond the court itself were the exciting surroundings of Edinburgh. The market places, the merchants booths, the craftsmens shops, the narrow closes, the narrow smelly wynds and the magnificent houses of the nobility and the rich merchants, side by side with the hovels and wretchedness of the ragged populace, were all a constant source of fascination to me. Mostly built on the steep rock on which the castle stood the city was a veritable maze, which it took months of exploration to get to know. The numerous pigs, hens, cows, horses and other livestock, which were kept in the back alleys and often spilled over into the main streets, amongst the teeming anthill of humanity, added further variety to an ever-changing scene, which I came to know well and never failed to enjoy.

Our duties as pages were not onerous. We were expected to run errands, fetch and carry small packages, or messages, and dance attendance on our appointed lords and ladies at certain times of the day, or when we were on special duties.

"Fetch me a page," was the general cry, which would send those of us appointed for duty that day or hour, scurrying in turn to obey the command to take a message to some other corner of the castle, or to fetch so and so, or bring such and such. In that one had an ear to the inner comings and goings, both the trivial and affairs of state, it was always interesting. Yet I confess that I found observing the affairs of the grooms and serving wenches, or the doings of the merchants, or the skilled work of the craftsmen in leather, or precious metals, almost as absorbing. The work of the skilled blacksmiths turning out complete suits of armour to fit different sized individuals, or producing an intricate inlay on a sword blade, a battle axe, or an individual helm or breastplate was also something that I always found of interest.

In our off-duty moments, which were plentiful enough, we mostly had our own activities to follow. After I had come to know the Castle itself and then the city I began to explore the countryside outside. The famous hill, King Arthur's Seat and the nearby Crags, the Nor' Loch and the charcoal burners in the Valley of Dean were all explored in turn. An occasional expedition might be made even further afield to the busy fishing port of Leith on the Firth of Forth. There the fishwives were always a fascinating sight, hard at work from dawn onwards with flashing knives gutting the daily catch brought in by the fishing fleet for sale later in the day in Edinburgh. But hunting or falconry in the fields and wooded country round Craigmillar, or further afield, whenever the King and his nobles disported themselves was an ever welcome break in the routine.

I soon found successors to Alistair and Dougal in the king's chief huntsman, a lean dark featured Lowlander, one Robert Johnstoun, and in the chief man-at-arms, William Irvine, a red faced martinet. Of all those at court, however, I must acknowledge my undoubted debt of thanks to him who proved one of the greatest influences on my life, Jamie Douglas, the court fool. Fool, poet, wit, dancer, contortionist, scholar and mystic, as well as perhaps more than a little mad, I found Jamie the most interesting repository of knowledge I ever encountered.

Fluid and flowing in movement, almost languid at first appearance, Jamie could without warning become a sudden whirlwind of motion, making fantastic leaps and pirouettes, as if his limbs were double-jointed and his legs pure whipcord and muscle. Although excelling at avoiding a quarrel, with an amazing ability to turn away all wrath and convert it into laughter by use of a polished epigram, or brilliant unexpected turn of phrase, he could as readily, when required, produce a merciless and cutting comment which would make the recipient writhe as though beneath the lash of a whip. Yet by the use of mime, he could also hold his audience enthralled without speaking a word.

Nor was he afraid of any man, whatever his strength or degree. I once saw him deal easily with Tom Hogg the giant blacksmith in the Haymarket, famed for his muscle and wrestling prowess, laying him senseless for beating his apprentice without cause in a fit of rage. On another memorable occasion I saw him defeat an attack by the Earl of Morton armed with his two-handed sword and angered at some careless phrase by simply using a poker from the fireplace. He disarmed him with seeming contemptuous ease and poked him in the stomach so that he puked up all his evening's meat and wine and took to his bed for a full day to recover. Admittedly both these men were in their cups at the time, but that merely made them the more to be feared in the eyes of everyone present bar Jamie.

"Use a man's strength against him, Iain," he used to advise me. "Now. See. When I attack you so, with the knife held high, all you need to do is take hold of my arm, so, lean back, twist and turn your back to help me on my way."

Suiting his actions to his words he would then cartwheel lightly over my turned back and landing on his feet would face me again, ready for a repetition until I was sufficiently skilled to pass his exacting standards. Were one not to attain these he was capable of blistering phrases which spurred the recipient on to redoubled efforts to please him, hard taskmaster though he was. On the whole, however, he must in the main have been pleased with me for I was undoubtedly one of the few people he seemed to bother with at court. Almost everyone else from the King, my father, himself to the lowliest scullion, he treated with the same offhand, careless, languid manner, neither giving, nor taking offence until the mood was on him, when no person was safe from the actions or words of the licensed court fool.

"Tumbling and dance are forms of art too little studied in these crude times, Iain," he told me solemnly on one occasion. "One day they will be more fully appreciated. Meanwhile I must take what weak vessels I find, and do my best to turn them into something more polished. You have the seeds in you, at least."

With that he did a couple of handsprings away from me and half-turning his back challenged me to wrestle with him. Of course, inevitably, I landed flat on my back and half winded on the thickly rush strewn floor of the chamber where he conducted his wrestling and tumbling practice.

"Away to your Saracen serving wench in the kitchens, Iain," he chided me mockingly. "If you cannot do better than that you had as well chatter away to her in her heathen tongue rather than waste the time here of the only honest man in Scotland. Although why you waste your time with her I cannot imagine since even if fair for a blackamoor she is hardly well favoured."

"It gets me some tasty morsels I wouldn't see otherwise," I confessed truthfully enough to make him laugh.

Although he often used my fondness for the Saracen cook as a weapon to belabour me with I am not sure there was not an element of jealousy behind his banter. While he could speak Latin and Norman French and the Gaelic, like most of those at court, he was not able to converse in the Saracen tongue beyond a few of the laboured phrases in common use. On the other hand with a natural facility for mimicry and an ear for strange tongues and accents, which I had early discovered, I had soon picked up the speech bandied between the fair skinned Saracen cook and the various Nubian scullions kept at the court, as was the general practice of the day. After listening to their chatter for some weeks I had found myself gradually able to join in with them, much to their surprise and everyone else's, but also greatly to my benefit in choice titbits from the kitchen. Thus, quite accidentally, I added at least a smattering of the language to my native Erse or Gaelic and to the court Latin and Norman French, which, of course, were all spoken at Beaulieu and in which naturally enough I was already fluent.

All this, of course, was only after I had been some months at court and had learned my way around. During the first few weeks I suppose I was homesick occasionally for Bealieu, but on the whole life was too full of exciting new experiences to miss my old home greatly. As the King's acknowledged natural son I was also accorded a great deal more respect, at least by some, than I had ever known at Beaulieu. Admittedly this was mainly from those whose opinion I did not greatly value and who, as I now realise, hoped for some return in course of time.

To the majority of the multitudinous court retinue, however, I was just another page and was generally treated as such: a cross between the quality and the servants themselves. Few saw any reason to curb their tongues in the presence of youngsters our age. As a result I saw a fascinating mirror image of the court life.

I was soon privy to all the undercurrents of feeling, the carefully hidden resentments, the long cherished grudges and feuds between individuals and families, the insubordinate murmurings as well as the simple likes and dislikes most people were careful to hide from their equals. I was also soon aware of the amazingly complex hierarchy, or pecking order, which existed at every level with everyone seemingly striving to maintain their position. Even my Saracen kitchen wench held herself above many of her compatriots she judged her inferiors. Almost the only person seemingly immune from this ambition for rank and position was my friend and mentor Jamie Douglas, the court fool.

Inevitably it was not long before I encountered James Macdonnel, and at first I thought I had misjudged him for he greeted me by name readily enough with something of his old charm, even if tinged with a slightly distant hauteur, as he no doubt felt befitted a squire of eighteen months standing addressing a newly appointed page.

"Ah, Iain! So they've sent you down here at last?" he greeted me, rather as if the Frasers had finally got rid of a tiresome incubus.

His next words, however, revealed something of the deep-seated resentment he still felt.

"Well, I trust you will keep better company here than low born curs like the huntsmen and men at arms at Beaulieu."

This slur on Alistair and Dougal was more than I could stomach and unthinkingly I said the one thing calculated to cause him to reveal his true feelings.

"They never said anything, James," I replied, loyal to my old friends and trying at the same time to reassure him. "Nor did I. No-one said a word, I promise you."

It was as if he had dropped a mask. His face paled, then suffused crimson with rage. In an instant, instead of the distantly haughty smile, there was a maliciously sneering curl of the lips and this time there was no mistaking the look of hate in his eyes. His hand dropped to the knife at his belt and for a moment I really thought he meant to attack me there and then. However, the timely approach of some of my contemporaries helped him to regain control of himself with an obvious effort.

"I simply don't know what you're talking about," he snapped. "But you always were a stupid blabbermouthed little fool and I might have known you wouldn't change."

With that he swung on his heel and left me without another word, As far as I was concerned it was an unpleasant reminder of a shattered friendship, which I now saw was past repair. Thereafter, as if by mutual agreement, James Macdonnel and I took care to avoid each other whenever possible. This did not prevent him sneering openly whenever we were in each other's company and on such occasions he seemed unable to prevent himself making spiteful remarks calculated to wound.

"I see the little Bastard is still keeping the company of churls and fools," he observed to a group of fellow squires for instance on seeing me pass after taking my leave of Jamie. "He was ever fawning about the men-at-arms and the stables at Beaulieu. More the behaviour of a groom's bastard I would have thought."

Although I pretended to ignore this and similar barbed sallies it was difficult to curb my tongue, more especially as I knew such comments were not confined only to my hearing. I was aware from comments passed by others that they had overheard similar remarks, but I soon came to realise that they did nothing to enhance his stature, indeed very much the opposite. Some of the more open-minded of his equals I gathered laughed openly at what they saw had become almost an obsession and no doubt this only made matters worse. It was I, myself, however, who fed the flames of his hatred by an ill-considered jest.

It happened that several of the smaller pages, myself included, took it in turns to serve as acolytes under the sacristan in the side chapel reserved. amongst other formal occasions, for the vigils of prospective knights. This chapel had a small tower and belfry, seldom used except on feast days. The bell was thus kept mute with a leather tongue covering the clapper save for such special occasions. This led to several of the more adventurous acolytes playing at swing on the bell rope, which when not in use hung up to one side or other of the chapel.

"It should be possible to swing from the Saint's niche on one side of the chapel to the other," remarked Alan Fraser thoughtfully, measuring the distance with his eye.

It was one of our tasks on feast days to climb the tiny narrow spiral stairs inside each corner column which led to the alcoves on each side of the chapel above the altar in order to light the candles which stood at the feet of the saints. (*Such narrow spiral stairs are still common inside the columns of many old churches and cathedrals. Like the cleaning of chimneys right up top the 19th century, lighting the candles in such niches appears to have been regarded as suitable work for a child. No doubt, however, the smallness of many of these spiral stairs was dictated by the size of the columns inside which they were built.*) The bell rope, when not in use, was looped back over a retaining hook on one or other side of the chapel. It hung temptingly close to the niches.

"Someone would have to release the rope and swing it up to the person standing by the Saint," I said thoughtfully as the idea took root in my mind. "Suppose you unhook it and pass it to me."

In a few minutes I was in position in front of St Paul. Alan was swinging the rope to me and someone else was keeping watch at the chapel door.

"Here goes," I cried, as I grasped the bellrope firmly and stepped off into space.

After an exhilarating swing through the air clean across the chapel I found myself in the other recess staring St Peter in the face. Reaching out a hand to support myself, I turned round nimbly and without a second's hesitation launched myself outwards again and after another thrilling swing through the air I was standing back where I had started in front of St Paul.

"Oh, well done, Iain," applauded Alan. "My turn now."

I slid down the narrow spiral stair in a manner which would have drawn a reprimand from Father Benedict had he seen me, for it was a quick way to ruin one's clothes and sandals. In a few moments Alan was in position and I was about to swing the rope to him when a warning cry from the doorway brought matters to a halt.

"Look out! Father Benedict's coming."

When he appeared in the doorway a few moments later we were all about our tasks with an air of conscious rectitude which should have warned him that we were up to some mischief, but apart from a dry remark about our sudden attention to our duties he made no other comment. It was, however, not until the following day that Alan was able to have a swing and then, mistiming his return slightly, he nearly brought St Paul crashing to the ground as he seized him instinctively for support. Fortunately after a perilous moment, while the Saint rocked backwards and forwards alarmingly on his plinth with boy and statue teetering, it seemed to us below, on the verge of destruction, Alan reached out a hand to grasp the edge of the alcove itself and regained his balance as well as steadying the statue.

"That was a close thing," he commented soberly, still ashen-faced, when he came down the spiral stairway. "Another inch or two and St Paul would have been lying in fragments on the chapel floor. And how would we have explained that to Father Benedict, I ask you? That's the last time I try that game."

Neither he, nor any of us, commented on his likely fate in those circumstances with the heavy plaster statue falling on top of him. The thought was sufficient to deter any others from trying to emulate the feat. But I had tasted the thrill of flying through the air and felt the urge to try it yet again. It was only a week or two later, when a suitable opportunity arose, that I persuaded Alan to pass me the rope again and I repeated the feat. The time after that I surpassed myself by leaping for the rope from the Saint's niche and then swinging across to the other side without assistance. I then found it was possible to swing the rope so that it hooked itself into position behind the retaining hook on the other side of the chapel. This was not its accustomed place, but few people were likely to notice the difference and thereafter when the coast was clear I made a practice of swinging across the chapel to the mixed delight and terror of the other acolytes who saw me. Despite some close shaves I was never caught, though on at least one aoccasion Father Benedict was only seconds away from catching me in mid-air.

"What are you doing there, Iain?" he demanded, seeing me standing beside St Paul in his niche, having just looped the rope round its hook.

"Just removing the stub of the candle, Father." I replied, inwardly quaking at the narrowness of my escape.

He appeared satisfied with my reply, but I felt he could hardly have missed the sly amusement or open guilt on the faces of some of the others. Perhaps it was only that they were obvious to me from my vantage point and doubly obvious because of my own guilty conscience.

"You're bound to get caught one of these days, Iain," Alan protested afterwards. "If you keep on doing it there's nothing more certain."

I never was caught and the reason I stopped in the end was nothing directly to do with Father Benedict. It was really the result of a totally hare-brained action on my part. Like so many youngsters of that age, I was continually trying to outdo my previous efforts and soon after this narrow escape I decided that nothing would suit me but to try swinging between the Saints' niches at night when only the candles were alight. The idea grew on me until I knew that I would not be content until I had achieved it or failed in the attempt.

"You're mad, Ian," Alan protested, when I revealed the ideas to him. "You'll break your neck for sure and I'll have nothing to do with it."

The chief drawback was that the candles were only lit when a service of some sort was about to be held and then the acolytes were under the gaze of others almost all the time and there was always someone in authority in the chapel. The only occasion we had the chapel to ourselves was in the mornings. Finally it struck me that one of the few occasions when it might be possible to gain free acccess to the chapel at night was just before the start of a young knight's vigil prior to gaining his spurs. Then the candles were lit in each Saint's niche a good hour or more before the young novice came to spend his vigil on his knees before the altar. It had to be the machinations of Fate that the novice about to undergo his all-night vigil turned out to be James Macdonnel, although I was quite unaware of this at the time. Nor would I have given it a second thought had I known of it. It was even more unfortunate, of course, that for reasons of his own he should have chosen to arrive early just as I had made sure that no-one was present and had slipped into the spiral stairway below St Paul.

I was wearing a light cloak, for the night was cold and we had just been singing at evensong. It may be that the brushing of the cloth against the narrow walls of the stairway deafened me to anything else. for when I emerged at the top I was startled to see a dark figure moving below me. He passed behind the altar and seemed to me to pause there for a moment or two, but I could not see who it was or what he was doing, for I was afraid to lean forward in case I drew attention to myself. A moment or two later I was greatly relieved to hear footsteps retreating down the aisle and what sounded like the creak of the outer door opening and closing. I was sure that whoever it was had left and that I was now all alone. Accordingly I reached over and seized the bellrope and swung myself into the darkness.

What I had not allowed for was the effect of the cloak trailing behind me. The outflung hem swept across the candle wick behind me and extinguished it. Guided by the remaining candle on the opposite side I swung straight across the chapel, but a frightened shriek from the darkness beneath me almost made me miss my long accustomed aim. Then, in reaching for my handhold on the edge of the alcove, I neatly extinguished the other candle, plunging the chapel into total darkness. I did not hesitate, however, and, knowing my way from long practice, once beside the statue of the saint, I slid down the stairway with scarcely a pause. In the utter blackness of the chapel I was aware of a rush of feet and a figure throwing open the side door and vanishing from sight. Intent on making good my own escape I followed as fast as I could, pausing only to close the door,

"Where have you been?" demanded Alan suspiciously, as I joined him in our common room, still panting from my exertions.

"I did it," I replied triumphantly

"I don't believe it," he answered, knowing at once what I meant.

Despite his reply, it was obvious enough that he did believe me, and it was barely a moment later that my story was confirmed in an entirely unexpected manner by none other than Father Benedict himself. He appeared in the doorway of our common room just seconds after I had removed my cloak looking distinctly worried and upset, which in such an even tempered man was unusual to say the least.

"Have any of you been in the chapel in the past few minutes?" he demanded abruptly.

"We've all been here since returning from Evensong, Father Benedict," replied Alan, covering for me with an ingenious half-truth, since my return was somewhat belated to say the least.

"Well, anyway, I need one of you to come and light the candles in front of the Saints in the Chapel. They've both gone out," he explained, "You Iain, you'll do. Come with me."

With frown on his usually unfurrowed brow he turned away and I leaped to my feet and followed him back the way I had so recently come.

"I can't understand it," he muttered to himself, apparently forgetful of my presence. "Why should the bellrope have been hanging free in the middle of the chapel?"

On hearing this I realised that, of course, in my haste and in the pitch darkness I had forgotten to loop the bellrope over the hook at the side of the chapel. I felt a momentary qualm, but there was nothing to be done about it, and I followed him obediently to the door of the chapel. Once there he led me into the robing room and lit a taper, which he handed to me.

"Off with you now, Iain," he said. "And light the candles. I can't think how they both came to go out."

I took the taper from him and obediently lit the candles in the niches. I noted that the bellrope had now been neatly hung in its accustomed place, but there was no sign of James Macdonnel, although by this time he should have been starting his vigil. I felt it wiser not to ask any questions and my unwonted silence might well have raised Father Benedict's suspicions, had he not been clearly preoccupied with his own thoughts. It was thus not until I returned to our common room that I was enlightened, for by then it seemed almost everyone had heard the story.

"You'll be interested to know Iain," Alan announced dramatically on my return. "James Macdonnel claims he saw an angel fly through the air above the altar and the movement of its wings blew out the candles!"

I must have looked at him in total amazement for at the sight of

immediate range of Whitehall, where the sun is shining brightly, combined with the traditional British feeling of throwing aside the trammels of convention when crossing the Channel. This is a heady combination even capable of undermining the British Army's sense of order and discipline. Of course it may just be that out of sight of Whitehall even the senior officers feel more relaxed. These feelings have a way of percolating downwards through the ranks. Inevitably, however they stop short at the RSM who doesn't care a damn for Whitehall and doesn't worry too much what his officers get up to, but does believe strongly in maintaining military order and discipline in the ranks.)

It was thus after a gap of several years that I again encountered James Macdonnel.

"I saw an old friend of your's a few minutes ago," Alan informed me one day with a grin. "If you care to walk a few yards you can see him for yourself. He's riding in to make his presence known to your father."

I walked down the row of tents and turned the corner in time to see James Macdonnel, his red hair shining in the sunlight, pacing to and fro on his charger as he waited for an audience with the King, my father. He still had the same aura of graceful careless charm, but now there was something else. After a few moment's study I realised that the old impatient tilt of the mouth at individual stupidity had given way to a permanent sneer of discontent with the world in general. The slight petulance of old was now a haughty disregard for others, combined with a glitter in his eye which mirrored a firm resolve to ride roughshod over them whenever they got in his way. Seeing him again in this way in an unguarded moment while he was still unaware of my scrutiny I realised with a sudden lift of my spirits that this man no longer had any power to sway my feelings. I saw too that the man was merely a natural extension of the boy I had known years before although at the time I had been blind to his obvious faults. Now magnified in manhood they stood out clearly, and the old surface charm, which had always blinded me to them could no longer conceal his inner shallow selfishness and ruthlessness.

The years might have changed my feelings, for in the interval I had grown from a boy into early manhood, but I was soon to realise this was no two way matter. Perhaps he felt the intensity of my gaze, or it may merely have been pure chance, but suddenly, at a summons from within, as he dismounted and tossed the reins of his horse with a typical careless gesture to his groom, his eyes rose and caught mine. For a moment he stared disbelievingly at my dark brown face and careless eastern garb, then his eyes gleamed darkly and his face twisted in a spasm of pure hatred. With a visible effort he controlled himself and turned away to enter my father's tent.

"Phew! That was no loving glance he gave you," remarked Alan with an uneasy laugh. "You'd best watch out or that loon will go out of his way to do you harm. That was almost the same dagger-in-the-back look you got from Tiénné Roland the other day."

I was reminded of Dougal and Alistair's words after the death of the Great Boar when they had both echoed much the same warning. But the sun was warm on my back and I was young and hot blooded. The momentary shock of seeing such murderous hatred in another's face was easily enough shrugged away and Alan and I were soon talking of falconry and hunting the oryx. All the same I think I knew then that I had indeed an enemy who was full of malice and who would stop at little to do me harm. James Macdonnell's murderous glare reminded me forcibly of the same look I had seen reflected on Mohammed Phayeed's face just a few weeks earlier. For that matter Tiénné Roland, Phayeed's arch enemy, had also mirrored much the same look.

In this climate, it seemed to me, men readily reached boiling point and, with so much intrigue amongst the numerous conflicting forces, there were a great many life and death quarrels in progress in which it was only too easy to become involved. Both Alan and I had given Phayeed and Roland cause to dislike us and they were not men who readily forgave or forgot. Hassan, I recalled, had been convinced that the attacks by footpads had been inspired by Phayeed. Now I had the brooding presence of James Macdonnel to add to those who wished me ill. Palestine, the famous Holy Land, seemed to be a place where it was easier to make enemies than friends and where deep hatreds and opposing religions seemed to flourish everywhere; the one feeding the other like a weed flourishing on a dungheap. Just how far such hatred could affect a man and warp his mind I had yet to learn. (*Regrettably very little seems to have changed over the centuries and it would have been interesting to hear Gleneil's comments on the current situation in the Middle East.*)

Chapter 5

The Siege of Acre

Preparing to move an army the size of the Crusading forces we had gathered together at Tyre was a massive task. There could be no secrecy about it and indeed little attempt was made to prevent the Saracens learning our intentions. With spies all around us, for despite his protestations, even such outwardly supportive Moors as Mohammed el Phayeed, vowing his eternal admiration for the Normans, the Franks, the English and the Scots were undoubtedly in constant touch with the Saracen forces, as was indeed his arch-rival Tiénné Roland, whose business connections seemed to extend to every sphere of activity and amongst all manner and colour of men. To all intents and purposes we were surrounded by spies, but then it was also largely a two-way traffic and little that the Saracens did or planned was not quickly passed back to us by much the same channels.

In the event it had probably suited Saladin to withdraw to his fort at Acre which he had good reason to think was well nigh impregnable. So it was that after embarking once again on board ships and lengthy marching and a good deal of cursing, we found ourselves no longer quite so comfortably camped outside the walls of the massive fort of Acre. There what appeared to be about to become a lengthy siege, with all the boredom, alarms and minor battles that such affairs inevitably involve, had already started. It was not really my idea of warfare, but then I was still young and in the process of learning that many of the practical experiences in life were very different from the theories taught earlier.

If anything in our new camp the flies and the sand and dirt were worse than they had been in Tyre, apart from which we did not have the advantage of a town on our doorstep ready to supply us with all our needs. Admittedly there soon appeared merchants from goodness knows where, ready and prepared to supply most of our requirements. It was amazing how they could suddenly appear, apparently out of the sand. There was also, it was true, a certain interest at first in watching the erection of several large throwing engines, or catapults, some of which could fling a dead horse stinking with maggots several hundred yards through the air to land inside the mighty walls of the fortress. Yet the plain fact is that once you have seen a few such feats further repetition does not improve the spectacle. It soon becomes extremely boring, even if the old soldiers amongst us assured us that the constant repetition tended to wear away the resistance of the garrison apart from sometimes causing disease. Others swore that only good rugged boulders wearing away the wall were effective, or else tunnels undermining the walls, or rams beating against them. Yet others advocated the advantages of Greek Fire and similar devices, but it all seemed to me a long way from tilting at the ring in the courtyard of Beaulieu. I had to agree with those individuals, and precious few they were, who said that straightforward fire with bows and arrows was more likely to have effect than anything else. It seemed our own uncertainty was mirrored by our commanders themselves for they appeared unable to agree as to the best methods to be employed.

(*This sounds like the perennial problem in an army where the high command is divided and more especially where the forces commanded have not always been allies in the past. It also sounds like the eternal division in any army between those who are interested in mechanics and engineering and those who are more interested in tactics and battles. Modern armies of course are divided into different corps for precisely this reason, so as to provide a body of experts in each field of warfare. At this time it seems everyone was a self-styled expert.*)

The normal methods of siege warfare were not much use in the desert. Tunnelling was difficult if not totally out of the question in the soft desert sand. For the same reason movable towers of a size suitable to attack the massive walls of the fort were a hopeless proposition. Movable shelters to protect the occupants from Greek Fire, molten lead and other such missiles were suggested by some enthusiasts who wished to undermine the walls. Others were in favour of using these to provide shelter for archers. In practice we soon relapsed into a routine whereby we kept up a desultory fire with our heavy catapults and made an occasional token attack, while the Saracens themselves replied with an occasional equally token sally. Although we had the advantage of sea power and virtual control of the sea with a number of vessels blockading the port, it was never too difficult for the Saracens to send in relieving vessels, usually under cover of darkness, to ensure they were kept well supplied. At the same time the Saracens had our camp virtually surrounded with the exception of a small coastal fringe. No large body of men could move without being instantly detected. The whole affair struck me as leisurely in the extreme, and not at all my idea of warfare.

On the other hand we were mere squires and it was not up to us to make policy or decide how the war should be fought. Like the bulk of our forces we were more concerned with whiling away the time in as pleasant a way as possible. Once again we took refuge in falconry and hunting the desert oryx, while others, including my Lord Dewrie, found their release in gaming and drinking.

There was a plateau Alan and I had discovered by a fortunate accident, having lost our way at the time, a few miles inland above a deep rocky pass known as the Wadi Halifa which wound its way through the desert down to the plain below Acre. Here we soon found there was always the chance of good falconry. Many of the sand grouse which congregated round the small springs in the desert each evening to drink flew to the shelter of a grove of olive trees which grew above the Wadi on the edge of the plateau. They provided incomparable sport for our falcons along with the bustards, which were also quite plentiful there, and occasionally we found an oryx or two on which we could let slip our hounds. This spot was rarely visited by anyone as far as we could see, for we seldom encountered more than a passing camel train usually led by only one man with his string of camels bound from one desert quarter to another. It was a seldom frequented area, probably because the effort of getting there through an area of rock strewn scrubland was enough to discourage those who did not know of its existence.

Since attending on my Lord Dewrie, as may have been gathered, was not a very taxing task and we were left with a good deal of free time, Alan and I spent many happy days hunting or hawking on this secluded plateau which we came to know well. With the lad Hassan in attendance and our hounds or hawks we had many a pleasant hour in the early morning or evening when the full heat of the day did not make exercise well nigh impossible. Since my Lord's horses and hounds required exercise, which he himself seldom gave them we felt virtuously that we were but doing what was necessary on his behalf, as well, it had to be admitted, as enjoying ourselves in the process.

(*Until the British army became a professional force, probably some time after the Korean War, British subalterns in overseas postings often had a very similar life. It was certainly not greatly changed up to the start of the 1939-45 war.*)

The general rank and file, however, were not so easily amused. There was little for them but dust, dirt and flies, with women and drink, when available, the only solace and disease and boredom the inevitable results. Boredom in turn led to quarrels, and we had trouble at times keeping Franks or Normans from the throats of English or Scots, or from each other, or indeed any of the other varied forces which made up the ranks of the Crusading army. Such tensions were probably inevitable and spread through the ranks to the Knights and nobility themselves.

During this period we suffered one or two sandstorms, which were exceedingly disagreeable experiences. The sky would darken and a wind would arise as if a storm was coming. Then suddenly the air would be full of sand, blotting out the sun and forcing man and beast to halt and take such shelter as was available until it was over. Alan and I were caught in one such storm in the open, but luckily it did not last for long, and we returned to the camp shaken, but unharmed. We were on horseback and fortunately we were accompanied by Hassan who recognised the signs. He persuaded us to dismount and turn our horses back to the approaching storm in the lee of a sand dune. We then covered their heads and ours with our cloaks and in this way escaped the worst. On another occasion when we were in the camp a storm lasted the best part of two days. It was impossible to leave the tents and the sand had drifted up the sides of them like snow. We were heartily glad that we were not caught in the open on that occasion.

Another extremely disagreeable experience was a swarm of locusts. This it seems is a not infrequent happening and we were told that every seven years or so the numbers increase to plague proportions. I can only say that it was a most extraordinary spectacle riding a horse and seeing this swirling black cloud approaching across the desert. At first we did not realise what it was until a few insects on the outer fringes of the swarm came near. The strange rustling noise their wings made as the swarm approached closer quickly grew to a menacing volume. We tried to gallop clear of it, but eventually we were engulfed in it and for a while it was like trying to ride through a swirling fog of flying black beetle-like insects, above an inch or more long, flapping and crawling over every exposed piece of skin or clothing. They had a particularly revolting metallic feeling, and the sensation of being in the midst of the swarm, with these flapping, crawling beetles everywhere was quite unnerving even if they were harmless enough.

Not surprisingly the experience drove the horses demented. We had to dismount and throw our cloaks over their heads to try to calm them, burying our own faces as well as we could in their necks, as they plunged and slithered around, for the ground was slippery with the winged bodies twitching and writhing underfoot. Once we were halted inside the swarm the sound of the insects' wings was deafening and the sensation of them crawling all over one's body was disgusting. Mercifully the swarm was not a large one and we were only on the edge of it so that it passed comparatively quickly. In a few minutes we could see the sun again. Soon afterwards, thankfully, the black mass was disappearing into the distance. We were able to brush off the remaining insects crawling on our clothing and remount our sweating horses. It may not have lasted very long but nonetheless it was a thoroughly loathsome experience. It was certainly not one I would care to repeat.

(Having driven through a swarm of locusts in an open Jeep, when we had to use the headlights to see the road and the wheels were skidding on their bodies crushed under the wheels I can sympathise with Gleneil. It must have been a very unpleasant experience indeed.)

The arrival at last in late June of King Richard, along with his Spanish wife, Queen Berengaria, and the bulk of the Crusading force did little to relieve the mounting tensions. More especially so as it did not seem as if they had made any great haste to join us. Rather than chance the winter storms in the Mediterranean they had overwintered in Sicily. Then leaving Messina in March they had stopped off at Cyprus on the way and, after a short campaign, had captured the island. Only then had they continued on to Tyre and so to Acre. The general feeling was one of anger that we had been kept waiting for their arrival for the best part of a year, while they had made no determined effort to join us.

King Richard himself was a man of commanding presence, a full two yards in height. He had hot challenging eyes above a nose, broken in some earlier combat, and a strong jaw. At first sight he seemed a regal figure, yet his was a restless nature, and he seemed hard put to it to remain still for more than a few moments on end. He would pace up and down while talking, and his words would often come with a rush. He was full of plans for attacking Saladin, many of which he wished put into action on the instant. Then at the slightest hint of opposition he would fly into an ungovernable rage in the face of which even his enemies quailed. Yet he was undoubtedly a brave fighter and a good general experienced in war, so that it was understandable enough why even those who disliked and distrusted him still let him take command in a campaign. His plans might sometimes seem close to madness, but often enough they were successful, perhaps from their sheer audacity, and despite his sudden rages and equally sudden smiles he was no fool. He might have his own favourites, such as Guy de Lusignan, who could do no wrong, but on the whole he was a good judge of a man. In matters of state, or politics, however, he would seldom give a direct ruling and his word could never be relied on. From bitter experience most of those he dealt with knew he was not to be trusted. Hence his nickname

Richard Yea and Nay. (*This description of Richard by a close observer is an interesting one. A psychiatrist today would probably label him a psychopath and the description of the abrupt mood swings and uncontrollable rages certainly point in that direction. On the other hand since he was brought up as a young man as a complete autocrat in charge of the whole of Aquitaine and then inherited the throne of England his behaviour is perhaps understandable enough. He was probably the victim of his own upbringing more than anything else. It might be argued that there was nothing wrong with him that a good nanny could not have put right.*)

It seemed to most of us that it was probably in an effort to relieve the steady build up in tension between the various factions amongst the Crusaders that soon after his arrival in June King Richard announced the holding of a Tourney in the desert some distance from our camp. The prospect of some action, even if only a token tourney, and jousting with the chance of some honour and glory, as well as a few broken limbs, was enough to raise everyone's spirits suprisingly. It may be too that the chance of breaking the heads of some of those to whom we had been forced to be stiltedly polite for some months while inwardly building up a fierce resentment was too good to miss. There was suddenly an almost carnival spirit in the air when the announcement of the meeting was made. (*The modern equivalent is probably the introduction of a series of football matches, although this often leads to more friction and rivalry than there was before. Of course exactly the same thing was almost certainly true of jousting tourneys. They also seem frequently to have ended in a free-for-all amongst the rival supporters. Even football hooligans it seems may lay claim to a long history.*)

For once Alan and I as squires found ourselves busy. We were soon superintending the men-at-arms and checking and double checking my Lord's arms and armour. My Lord's war horse had to go through his paces time and again until we were both satisfied that he at least would make no mistakes. His harness and that of my Lord had all to be checked and double checked yet again and oiled and polished and burnished until it shone as only silver and gold can, glinting brightly in the sun.

My Lord Dewrie himself was soon at work exercising himself with his arms, his lance, his double handed sword and his mace. As he practised in the heat of the sun with the sweat pouring off him we saw a different being to the casual gamester we knew so well. Underneath was a man of resolve and determination. In the matter of a week he had fined down from a portly figure of seeming advancing years into a tightly muscled man in the prime of life. The easy going master we had known was suddenly a cursing ball of energy, and we scarcely had a moment to ourselves.

"Come lads, this will not do," he snapped, when we eased for a moment in our efforts to match him at practice with sword and shield, or in other aspects of weaponry. "This is serious work lads, serious work. Go to it. Go to it."

The transformation was remarkable and, while we had to admire the man, we had little time for relaxation. He kept us and the men-at-arms hard at work and, had we had time to think about it, we should have realised that something more than a mere tourney must be behind it. For the moment however we were kept too busy to speculate and my Lord drove us hard.

Then abruptly the day of the tourney was upon us. We had helped the men-at-arms and camp followers struggle with tenting. Pavilions and a vast ring had been erected. From the site itself we could see the entrance to the Wadi Halifa and it was a source of continual frustration that we could also see the ridge beyond which lay what we always termed 'our' plateau, where we had enjoyed many halcyon days sport. Meanwhile an entire township of pavilions, tents and quarters for the horses and men had sprouted almost overnight in the desert.

Perhaps it was an overdose of the sun, used as I was to it by this time, or maybe something that I had eaten, but hardly had we finished our tasks and the whole place was alive with men and horses amidst the pennons, the banners and the silken bunting than I became sick with what we all knew descriptively as the Saracen Squats. (*A more modern equivalent would be Gyppy tummy or alternatively something like the Cairo/Gaza/Beirut/Algiers/Tripoli Trots depending on the nearest likely source. This particular bug sounds*

like the precursor and grand-daddy of them all, although the Romans
fighting in much the same area several centuries earlier probably had
exactly the same problem and this form of dysentery was probably much
the same as their's. All said and done men's innards haven't altered much
over the centuries and are constructed much the same regardless of
nationality. Some basic things really do not change greatly if at all.)

We all knew that to try to fight it was disastrous and completely
hopeless. Although a short term illness and regarded as something
of a joke, except by the current sufferers, it left one empty and shaky
after a day or two, but during that time you dared not move far. I
simply retired to my tent in the old camp amongst the remaining
camp followers and guards not involved in the tourney, and
remained near to a shovel ready to fill the next hole in the
ground. The boy Hassan, who seldom left my side, remained with
me in attendance. Over the months since I had acquired him,
he had proved himself a devoted and faithful servant to both Alan
and myself, but mainly, since I could speak many of his tongues,
to me.

It was thus that I missed the first day of the jousting when my
Lord Dewrie after acquitting himself well in a five-a-side melee, in
which he was only one of three left standing was so severely cracked
about the head that he was forced to retire to his bed. News of this set
back was relayed back to me by a messenger sent by Alan to assure
me that my presence would not be required in a hurry. It was thus
something of a surprise when I had still not fully recovered on the
third day to receive yet another message from Alan this time written
and sealed and sent by a Frankish knight retiring from the tourney
with a broken arm.

"If you are well enough meet me on the plateau by the olive grove
at dawn tomorrow without fail. Alan."

I was somewhat surprised at the rather peremptory and cryptic
nature of the message, but I assumed that perhaps he had been in a
hurry and with my lord Dewrie confined to his sick bed, felt like an
early morning hunt. While still not feeling perfectly recovered I
decided that by dawn all would be well and accordingly I made
arrangements to attend the meeting place. In the morning before

first light I was off and riding out with my favourite hound in attendance and the boy Hassan by my side,

There was a full moon casting shadows and lighting everything nearly as well as daylight, but the stars were still visible and I had no difficulty finding my way, which I knew almost as well as my trusty little Saracen stallion and for that matter my hound. As the first light of dawn was colouring the darkness of night into grey I surmounted the final ridge and saw a string of camels encamped near the olive grove. The single drover was still fast asleep by the remains of his camp fire.

From this point I could see far down on the plain below the fires of the tented township set up for the jousting twinkling in the darkness in serried rows. Of Alan, however, there was no sign at all at our usual meeting place, and I was soon mentally cursing him for sleeping in when he had made arrangements to meet me. It was still chill enough for me not to wish to stand around and I decided to move on to the grove of olive trees, in case there was any game lurking there which might be worthy of unleashing my hound

It was as I approached the trees that I first heard a strange sound I could not identify. It was for all the world like a giant's heart beat throbbing. I could feel a steady vibration which seemed to shake the air. At first I could not identify where it was coming from and then I realised it seemed to be from the Wadi Halifa itself.

I spurred my little Saracen steed forward to the edge and suddenly I saw the cause of the noise. Far below me the Wadi was filled with marching men. File upon file of black warriors were marching through the Wadi towards the unsuspecting Crusader camp in the desert. By the light of the torches carried by the leaders I could see they were the fierce Nubian warriors chosen by Saladin as the foremost troops in many of his battles and famed for their warlike qualities.

Already the foremost ranks had reached the opening of the Wadi where they were spilling out into the desert. At least two thousand more, it seemed, were behind them. It was impossible to make more than a wild guess at their numbers, but it seemed clear to me that the pick of the Crusading forces encamped unsuspectingly in the plain below would soon be overwhelmed, unless something was done at once. As I looked down the steep scree covered slopes at the masssing files of Nubian warriors below me, something about the scene reminded of the cliffs above the Bealieu Firth where we had often played as boys. In the instant a plan came to me.

"Come with me, Hassan," I cried, and whirled my horse round.

I set my heels into his flanks spurring as fast as possible for the camel encampment closely followed by Hassan. The camels, as usual, were loosely tied together with a plaited leather rope, and I wasted no time in running down the line slashing each head collar as I ran so that the line remained intact. When I had finished amidst the snorts of the roused camels and the sleepy yells of their keeper I was left holding the end of fifty feet or so of rope

Leaving it to trail behind me and the cursing camel keeper to sort out his snorting scattering beasts, I remounted and rode as fast as I could for the edge of the cliff. There I leaped from the saddle and, with Hassan's help, tied the rope securely round the nearest olive tree to the edge of the cliff. I then looked over and tossed the end down. With dawn now fast upon us and the light improving with every moment I was relieved to see that the rope's end lay some distance down beyond where the scree slope ended. I hoped it would be enough for what I had in mind. Anyway I decided it would have to do and I would soon know if I had judged it well or not.

Turning my game little stallion I galloped back a hundred yards or more along the cliff edge. Tossing the reins to Hassan I leaped off his back and looked down. The ranks of the Nubian warriors were now plain to see. Several hundred of the foremost had passed through the end of the Wadi, but seemingly endless numbers still marched swiftly down the rock strewn pass. There was no time to waste and no time to measure the dangers.

"Wait for me with the horses at the end of the rope" I said to Hassan.

Then, taking a deep breath, I leaped out over the edge of the cliff and started running with giant strides, as fast as I could, at an angle across the scree face, making a line as far as possible for the middle of the rope hanging over in front of me. With each stride I felt the rock face start to move and give beneath me, and I leaped as fast as I could for another foothold before I was sucked down with the moving rocks. My gaze was fixed on the rope hanging down in front of me. In the final strides I was convinced I had misjudged it and would miss it altogether. Then in the last seconds, as I was sure I was losing ground too fast to hope to reach the rope, a providentially placed short face of hard rock gave me a solid foothold again, and I continued on my way slightly upwards while the scree slid and rolled beneath my feet with an ever growing roar as the landslide I had set in progress took hold beneath me.

I just managed to catch hold of the extreme end of the rope with a final convulsive leap as I felt the ground disappearing beneath my feet and glimpsed nothing but empty space ahead. For an agonising moment I swung one handed into space. Then with a convulsive jerk I had hold with both hands and started climbing hand over hand. Below me the sound of the rocks rolling down the cliff mounted to a mighty roar, which I was later told could be heard in the Crusader's camp like the sound of thunder.

I felt an immense satisfaction at having I was almost sure thwarted the attack on the Crusader's camp. How much damage I had done I could not be sure, but I felt certain that I must have caused a good many casualties amongst the army of Nubians as well as at least partially blocking the pass through which they were hoping to attack. At the very least I was sure I must have delayed matters so that the Crusader's encampment would have time to prepare themselves.

Looking up above me I could see Hassan's head outlined darkly against the sky leaning over the edge his teeth gleaming white as he shouted encouragement. Then I started to climb. Although the length hanging down was not much more than thirty feet long I was feeling the effects of my exertions and I took some time to climb it, stopping from time to time to see if I could pierce the clouds of dust which eddied up from below and obscured everything from view. I was still looking down when I reached the top and this was a big mistake. I felt my shoulder seized and something heavy hit me on the side of the head. I was just conscious of being dragged over the edge and for a brief second I was aware of a somehow vaguely familiar voice:

"Now we have the little bastard!"

Then a bright light seemed to split my skull open and blackness descended on me. The next thing I was mindful of was the smell of camel dung. Then a foot prodded me in the ribs and I was aware of a sharp pain in my head and the sound of someone groaning. After a moment I realised the person groaning was me. As my senses partially returned I discovered that I was lying behind a line of camels with a villainous looking Moor poking me in the ribs with his foot.

"So this is the little Infidel who caused such havoc is it?" demanded another voice.

"He is nothing much to look at," added another.

Gradually a number of dark faces bending over me swam into my gaze and I realised that I was an object of interest to several Nubian guards who stood round me in a half circle. I could see no sign of Hassan or my horses.

"Anyway you shall have a reward for capturing him," the first speaker, who was clearly the leader, announced, addressing the Moor, who had been kicking me. "That at least should make up for having to round up your camels. Meanwhile we will take three of your beasts for our own use. You will be well paid for your trouble."

I was still barely conscious for I had not even appreciated that my hands were bound to my sides. Only some moments later, when I was ignominiously picked up and slung on the back of a camel like a piece of baggage, did I begin the realise my plight. The knowledge that I was now a prisoner of the Saracens and my likely fate did little to improve my aching head. Nor could I help feeling that there was something badly wrong. I was sure Hassan would not have deserted me, nor I felt certain was it his voice I dimly recalled just before I was hit, but such was my confused state of mind that I could no longer even remember the words I had heard.

I have known the same thing since with blows on the head. The mind plays strange tricks, and there is nothing to be done but wait to see if time will provide the answer. As I jolted backwards and forwards with the movement of the camel, however, it suddenly came to me. The voice I had heard as I reached the top of the cliff just before the blow on my head had surely been speaking in Norman French and something about it had been strangely familiar. It was not the Saracens who had laid me unconscious, but someone on our own side who had either left me for dead or to be captured. The trouble was that, try as I could, the memory of who it was would not come to me. Every time I thought I could put a name to the voice my mind seemed to become a blank. At the time I was infuriated that I could not recall this one all important point. I almost wept with frustration during that seeming interminable camel ride, but the end result was the same. I was sure that I knew who my attacker must have been, but I could not for the life of me recall who it was.

I daresay that I was only half conscious for much of that seemingly interminable ride. I do recall being passed like an inanimate piece of baggage into a boat of some kind and then transferred to another for by then it was dark and the salt spray from the sea splashed my face at one point and brought me out of the coma into which I had more or less relapsed. I can recall struggling feebly and being thrown contemptuously onto a pile of what I think must have been netting for there was a strong smell of fish. Throughout most of the journey, however, I was barely aware of what was happening.

It was bright sunlight when I next came to my senses. At first I could only feel the motion of the boat. Then I felt the boards below me and the ropes binding my arms to my body. A spasm of pain brought me fully awake as I moved my head incautiously. My skull behind my left ear was exceedingly tender and I could feel it throbbing whenever my head moved that way. I took care to ease my head onto my right side and keeping my eyes half closed against the glare of the sun I tried to work out where I was.

I felt sick and weak, but at least I was now able to think back more clearly even if the past hours remained only a hazy recollection. I remembered with a feeling of elation the reckless run down the scree face and the thunderous sound of the rock fall that had followed. I had a vivid memory of the clouds of dust swirling up from the Wadi floor, and I knew with a fresh thrill of satisfaction that I must have at the very least destroyed the Saracen's hopes of a surprise attack on the Crusaders' camp. Then I remembered the blow on the head, and I wondered with a sick feeling of betrayal whether Hassan had been responsible. Finally faint memories of a sentence in Norman French came back to me. The confused memories made my head ache and I relapsed into unconsciousness once more.

When I finally awakened again I felt a great deal more clear-headed. Looking around me I realised I was lying against a pile of netting thick with fish scales. On the other side deck planking obscured my view. Evil smelling water swilling to and fro around my feet and legs indicated that I was in the hold of a fishing vessel. Looking skywards I could see a mast and some rigging. Above that as I looked I saw a tower pass, which seemed faintly familiar. At the same moment there was a pattering of feet on the decking and I hear commands shouted and the grating of timber on stone. The boat's movement ceased, and I realised we were alongside a quay. I could see the tower clearly now, and recognised it only too well. The flag with the crescent on it was that flown by Saladin from the principal tower of Acre. With a sick feeling in the pit of my stomach I realised that I was inside Acre itself.

It was then the reality of my situation hit me, and I realised that as a prisoner of the Saracens I could expect little mercy. Memories of stories I had heard of their treatment of prisoners entered my mind unbidden, and I felt a sense of utter frustration and hopelessness. Yet I was determined not to give way however bad things might seem.

It was not long before I was put to the first test. A large bearded Moor appeared and looked down at me.

"Are you awake yet, little devil's spawn?" he demanded, prodding mein the ribs with a horny foot.

I gave no sign of life and he grunted disgustedly and reaching down hauled me over his shoulder like a sack. I was hard put not to groan as a spasm of agony lanced through my head like a red hot knife, but I managed to stay limp and through half-closed eyes took in as much of my surroundings as possible. It was but a few steps to the quayside, for the boat in which I had been lying was no more than a small fishing skiff, such as regularly ran the gauntlet of the Crusaders' fleet blockading the port of Acre.

At the quayside I was bundled across the back of a donkey like a bag of merchandise and without further ado was led along the quay and through the streets of the fortress. It was a hot and stinking progress, but news of my capture did not seem to have spread far. Hardly anyone paid any attention to me as I was borne through the streets like any other baggage. It was both humiliating and in a way reassuring. If I was not worthy of notice perhaps news of the landslide in the Wadi Halifa might not yet have reached Acre.

I was unable to get much idea of our progress bent double over the back of the beast, but when we halted I heard gates being opened and the sun vanished from sight as we entered a building.

"Here you are. Here's another Infidel prisoner for you," the Moor who had been leading the donkey announced,

A moment later I found myself hauled off its back and set unceremoniously on my feet, while a knife sliced through the ropes binding my arms. After lying bound and half conscious for almost a day I was in no state to stand and, had it not been for a restraining hand holding my shoulder, I would have crumpled to the ground.

"He doesn't look as if he'll give you much trouble," he added. "Doesn't look as if he's more than half grown."

Through half closed eyes I saw I was facing an elderly Nubian with a fringe of white hair and a long scar twisting one side of his face.

"Never trust them at any age," he replied, "Just follow me while I find a cell for him."

He turned and led the way down a stone passage with barred entrances. Some doors down he halted and fumbled with some keys before opening the door.

"Put him in there," he commanded.

I was thrust forward and with my captor's supporting arm removed my legs gave way. I sprawled face down on the filthy greasy stone floor. For a moment or two my senses left me again, but the cold dampness of the floor on my cheek brought me to my senses in a short while. The stink was nauseating. My nostrils quickly told that was no place to linger, and gathering my wits together with an effort I rose to my feet. It was a lengthy task and, apart from the stabbing pain in my head, I soon learned that in the past few hours I had acquired numerous other bruises and aches, the causes of which I did not know.

When eventually I was on my feet and leaning for support against the wall I began to take stock of my surroundings. There was a barred window high up through which the sun shone brightly and through which I could hear the bustle and noise of people at work. The door was barred and led onto a passage. There was no-one in the cell opposite, and I could hear no-one stirring on either side of me.

"Is there anyone there?" I called, but there was no reply.

In the cells the silence was absolute. It appeared that I was the only prisoner. Outside I could hear the bustle of the streets, the cries of vendors in the stalls in the bazaar, snatches of conversation from people passing in the street and the occasional sound of livestock, the braying of a donkey, the bleating of a goat, the crowing of a cockerel or barking of a dog. It was maddening to hear all these sounds so close at hand and yet be unable to see them. On the other hand I reflected that, even if I could see them, or even if I was outside and amongst them, I would still be an Infidel in the midst of a Saracen stronghold. On the whole I decided I was probably better off where I was, at least for the moment. The prospect of what was likely to come, however, did not give me any pleasure.

To fill in the time I examined my prison. Apart from the barred grill, which was about eight feet from the ground and the barred door through which I had been unceremoniously thrust it was a dank stone walled pen about six feet across and ten foot long by ten foot high. The floor was bare, but slimy underfoot with stale excrement and urine. There were two hooks on one inside wall about six feet up and six feet apart and two further hooks below them a foot or so off the ground. Beneath them the floor was particularly stinking and it did not require a great deal of imagination to see their purpose.

I had no time for much more than this cursory examination of my prison before I heard an inner door opening and the jangling of keys followed by voices.

"How long has he been here?" an angry voice demanded. "Why wasn't I told of his arrival?"

"He has not been here long," was the sullen reply. "I was going to let you know as soon as you returned. What's all the fuss about anyway? He's nothing more than a half grown beardless lad."

"Just that the governor himself has demanded that he be brought before him for sentence as soon as possible," came the unpromising reply. "Half grown and beardless or not, they say he killed over five hundred of the Nubian Guard with another five hundred or more suffering broken limbs."

"There has to be some mistake," the other grumbled stopping at the doorway to select the key. "Look at him for yourself. He couldn't kill one Nubian Guard let alone five hundred."

"They say he started a rockfall above the Wadi Halifa," explained the first speaker, who turned out to be a tall fair skinned Moor with a greying beard. "The Nubian Guard were marching through it at the time to attack the Crusader's camp."

"Oho," muttered my gaoler. "It was a bad day for him when he let himself be captured then. The governor will not welcome the loss of so many of Saladin's picked Guard."

I was more than inclined to agree with him, but I saw no profit in letting them know that I understood their tongue so I merely remained standing when they entered the cell.

"Come with us," ordered the grey bearded Moor,

When I made no move the scarred gaoler seized my arm.

"Come on you little vermin," he grunted, making his meaning unmistakeable with a sharp push in my back.

Marched between the pair of them with the gaoler gripping my arm I walked up the corridor and out of the main entrance to the cells. Here, in the hallway, was the main entrance through which I must have been brought earlier as a largely inanimate burden over the shoulder of the seaman who had carried me. It all seemed as if it had happened long ago and to someone else. I must have been still suffering from the effects of the blow on my head or perhaps it was the effect of the powerful sunlight outside, or a combination of the two, but whatever the reason I began to feel as if I was apart from the proceedings and merely a spectator watching my gaolers march me down the street.

It was still with this peculiarly detached feeling that I found myself before an imposing arched gateway. This was opened by two liveried servants dressed in rich silks and armed with large scimitars.

"We have brought the prisoner to the presence of the Caliph as he commanded," announced the greybearded gaoler importantly.

Another liveried presence in the background came forward revealing himself as a bearded majordomo, who waved his hand onwards towards a flight of marble stairs.

"Follow me into the presence of his Highness," he commanded.

The marble stairs were cool underfoot and the palace, for such it clearly was, seemed shady and airy after the intense heat of the sun outside. Cunningly contrived shutters permitted rays of sunlight to enter and yet managed to provide shade and coolness. Fountains in the inner courtyard provided a welcome distraction from the heat of the sun. In ordinary circumstances I would have enjoyed the contrast between the inside of the marble palace and the throbbing sunshine and dust of the streets outside, but I was unable to avoid feeling a sense of dread at coming into the presence of the Governor of Acre. No-one in their right senses wishes to hear themselves sentenced to death.

The majordomo led us forward into a palatial room on the first floor where the inner windows were open to the courtyard and the sunlight after the shade elsewhere was dazzling. He bowed low and motioned to the two gaolers to bow also, but they were already doing so and the scarred one thrust me down to my knees. It did not require much effort to do so, but I did my best to scramble upright as soon as possible.

It was easy at first to overlook the man who sat in the throne in an alcove facing the doorway, but I realised his position gave him the opportunity to see each new arrival before they saw him. Dressed in a plain dark green silken robe and not above middle height he was not at first sight a particularly impressive figure, but his eyes had a peculiar intensity, and his voice when he spoke was deep and clear.

"So this is the Infidel who killed seven hundred or so of our finest Nubian Guard and disabled almost as many more," he said in the Saracen tongue, eyeing me keenly as he spoke.

I felt an upsurge of satisfaction at learning this news, but managed to keep my face impassive, and let my eyes wander round the room as if more interested in my surroundings than what was being said.

"I see he does not understand our tongue or he would realise the fate that lies in store for him," he continued. "Even though the rock fall he planned missed most of the troops and merely half blocked the Wadi Halifa he will still die tomorrow regardless."

I almost made the mistake of showing my surprise at these words directly contradicting his earlier statement, but realised in time that this was his intention and managed to continue my overt inspection of the room as if unable to understand a word. It seemed to have the desired effect for he went on, addressing my gaolers.

"A messenger from Mohammed el Phayeed informed us that the Crusaders would be encamped in the desert, and we sent two thousand of the Nubian Guard to overwhelm them," he explained. "But this young stripling, unaided, appears to have thwarted our plans. He does not seem capable of such a deed, but, be that as it may, he must suffer accordingly."

He then addressed me in passable Latin.

"What is your name?" he demanded.

"Gleneil, your highness," I replied, not sure quite how I should address him.

"You are an unfortunate young man," he said gravely. "You appear to have been betrayed by your own side and, had you not the blood of some of my finest Guard on your head, I would have felt inclined to spare you."

"All I know is that I was hit on the head and then captured, highness." I replied.

"You were found bound and unconscious by the camel driver whose rope you stole. He said you were left by someone mounted on a horse and wearing the sign of the cross," the governor replied impassively. "And, while I do not approve of taking advantage of treachery, the blood of many men is on your head. Accordingly I decree that you will suffer the customary fate tomorrow at dawn if the Council agrees."

He turned to my gaolers.

"Take him before the Council and inform them of my views," he commanded them. "But whatever their decision see that he is given food and drink. He has served his own side only too well and deserves to meet his God on a full stomach."

I liked the sound of the food and drink, but I was not too keen on the rest of his remarks, especially as I could not see the Council, whoever they might be, arguing much if the Governor of Acre, representative of the Great Saladin himself, had made his decision. Nor was I far wrong. When I was brought before them they turned out to be a group of Caliphs of varying ages, from greybeards to one young man not much older than myself. They had hardly heard the Governor's recommendation before they all started nodding their heads with varying degrees of intensity. All that is except for that one youngster of much my own age, who took the view that as treachery was involved by our side that they should not take advantage of it, and I should be let off with the chance of mortal combat on even terms instead of crucifixion, which of course we all knew was the usual fate for Infidels.

I was not sure whether this sounded a much better alternative, but it did not seem to have quite the inexorable inevitability of being nailed to a cross. Anyway the young Caliph in question was quickly shouted down, and, for his pains, was awarded the task of rising at dawn to supervise the punishment, So much for the chances of the Governor being overruled I thought as I was led away back to my cell. While I was all in favour of the young Caliph's objections and alternatives, I could see that next time the Council met he would think twice before stepping out of line.

When I had been led back through the streets and then locked in the same stinking cell again, the bearded gaoler, who was clearly in overall charge, himself brought me a trayful of food and a beaker of cool lemon juice despite the audible grumbling of his scarred underling.

"The Governor said he should be fed and given drink," he said. "And we will obey his orders, whether you like it or not"

I have to admit that the food, a light stew of freshly killed kid's meat and the lemon juice made me feel wonderfully recovered. I took my time over eating it and could feel new life returning to me all the time. The greybearded superior went further and provided me with a bowl of cool water and a cloth to wash my face and head. It was particularly pleasant to remove the dried blood from my face and hair and, although I could still feel a walnut sized lump on the side of my head, I felt immensely better as a result. By the time I had eaten and drunk and completed my ablutions I felt almost completely recovered; such is the power of recuperation of youth.

Even though to make up for such leniency the scarred gaoler then took a certain malevolent pleasure in chaining my wrists and ankles to the hooks on the wall, leaving me more or less suspended between them for the night I still felt greatly refreshed and almost myself again. It was not a comfortable position and the stench of my surroundings made it less so. On the other hand the alternative of trying to sleep on that wet and stinking floor was not much better.

I spent some time in profitless speculation as to who could have been responsible for my betrayal. That Mohammed el Phayeed was responsible for passing on news of the movements of our army did not surprise me greatly. Proving it would no doubt be more difficult. He would be sure to claim that it was all part of a conspiracy against him and that his enemies were responsible for such calumnies. However the nagging thought that someone on our side had hit me on the head and delivered me bound to the camel driver was another matter. I was sure that I could recall a voice speaking just as I was hit on the head, but the words and the name of the speaker eluded me, although inwardly I was certain it was familiar.

(*Research indicates that many readers ignore Prefaces and Introductions, preferring to start at Chapter 1. With this in mind, and to avoid a hiatus in the text, the account with which Gleneil opened the record of his life has been inserted here in the chronoligical sequence. The diligent reader will note that some editorial insertions have been added.*)

They came for me at dawn. I remember waking to the sound of

their voices approaching, for, in spite of everything, at some time during the long hours of the night I must have fallen asleep. The sour stink of stale urine and the feel of the dank walls against my almost naked body quickly brought me back to grim reality. Then the flickering light of their lamp casting weird shadows round the dungeon revealed them. They were three of Saladin's Nubian bodyguard, all specially picked men, six feet or more in height, with shoulders like the span of an ox. Each wore an unsheathed scimitar through the belt of his baggy breeks, above which, like me, they were naked. Their heavily muscled oiled torsos gleamed like metal in the lamplight.

"This infidel is little more than a child," grunted their leader contemptuously, using a heavy hammer to knock off the shackles which held me spreadeagled against the wall, chained by wrists and ankles alike.

"Yet he started the landslide in the Wadi Halifa which took five hundred or more of the Faithful into the arms of Allah and disabled as many more," growled one of his companions. "He deserves his fate and let us rejoice in it. May the jackals eat his bones."

"Ha. He prostrates himself in front of us," their leader chuckled, as my knees buckled and I fell forward onto the ground.

Tucking the hammer into his waistband he caught hold of my wrist and jerked me one-handed to my feet.

"Get up little dog's spawn," he jeered. "You've not got far to walk. Then you'll never need to walk again."

I made no reply for I saw no need to let them know I spoke their language and, truth to tell, I had been stretched so long between those shackles I had no need to feign faintness. Nevertheless, with the resilience of youth I could feel the blood coursing through my veins, giving me fresh hope as I was held upright and regained my balance.

"Come, you two. Take the little infidel between you and I'll take the lamp," commanded the leader impatiently. "If he won't walk you can drag him along between you."

Each of them obediently took a grip on my upper arm and lifted me effortlessly between them, scarcely conscious of my weight.

Outside the dungeon the air of the desert, laden as it was with the smell of camel dung and campfires, smelt sweet by comparison with that stinking interior. The stars were still clear against the steely sky, but a faint glimmering in the East indicated the first approach of dawn and in these parts it is not long from dawn to sunrise. It was only a short distance to the Castle gates where the guards were waiting to let us through a small postern, which they bolted and barred behind us,

Once in the open we moved at a fast pace, with my feet only touching the ground at intervals, suspended inertly between my two guards. Though I hung limply between them, I could feel my strength steadily returning. It was not long, however, before we halted abruptly.

"Here we are," grunted their leader impatiently. "And no sign of His Highness yet."

By then dawn was already appreciably lightening the sky and beside us I could see all too clearly the fate that was awaiting me. A cross of cedar wood freshly hewn, so that the fragrance permeated the air, stood at a point where the ground started to slope steeply down towards the plain of Acre. Below us the lights of numerous campfires glowed and flickered fitfully in ragged lines and already a stirring and murmuring could be heard as the Christian armies of the Third Crusade began to prepare for the dawn stand-to-arms. Behind us a similar low murmur like a giant hive of bees disturbed inside the towering Castle walls indicated that Saladin's army was likewise preparing itself, and the high notes of the Muezzin calling the faithful to prayer sounded as herald of the dawn.

"Ha. He faints at the sight of his fate," commented the leader scornfully, as I tripped on the rough ground when they set me roughly down.

Though I could see no possible chance of escape it struck me as no bad plan to encourage them to think me quite harmless and I drooped between the two guards still holding me as if I might indeed faint at any moment. Meanwhile the light was improving with every moment passing and I fancied I could even see the first faint glow of sunrise striving to rise and seal my fate.

Although I continued to feign faintness I could feel within me the mounting tingle of excitement I have always felt before any action. If my guards vigilance should lapse for a second I determined to seize my chance, despite the odds. As the moments passed and their boredom increased I had little difficulty in drooping miserably between them, letting them support my full weight, but all the time I was inwardly alert for any mistake they might make.

Then came the sound of galloping hooves growing rapidly closer. Within a few moments a white arab stallion reared to a halt in front of us and I saw the grey eyes and hooked nose of Haroun el Fahid the young Saracen Caliph appointed by the court the day before to supervise my crucifixion. Little older than myself, it was clear enough that he did not greatly relish the business in hand.

"When the sun rises," he commanded abruptly. "Let him meet his fate as has been decreed."

Wheeling his horse down the slope he remained only a few yards away with his back turned to the prceedings, gazing down defiantly at the massing forces of the Crusader's army lining up on the plain below facing the high castle walls of Acre. Several hundred yards behind us the Saracen trumpets sounded their outlandish wailing and from the serried ranks below came a sullen growl like the roar of a pack of lions at the familiar ritual about to take place in full view above them.

(*Since dawn has always been a favoured time of attack it has been inevitable that armies have stood-to over the centuries, ready to repel the enemy at the same unearthly hour. The same thoughts and feelings, edgy, scruffy, unshaven, sleepy and plain fed-up, as well as like as not miserable, soaking wet and scared stiff, must have been the lot of countless soldiers of every race and creed over the centuries in every major war and minor battle at this same usually ghastly time of day. It is after all a time of natural hiatus, the time of day when the beasts of the night, the foxes, the bats and the owls, the croupiers and night club managers are returning to their lairs for the daylight hours, while the early birds in search of worms, the milkmen on their rounds and the newsboys delivering the morning papers are just about to set out. The former group are exhausted by their night's work and looking forward only to bed. The latter are still only half awake have not yet achieved the state of mind, after the first worm, or jangling the first milk bottles, or throwing the first batch of papers expertly against a front door, when song or a whistle rises naturally from the inner bird, or man. It is not usually a time of day when the majority of the human race are at their best, even supposing at that hour they even feel they qualify as members. With the prospect of imminent action ever present the state of mind is not improved. It is then that feelings of animosity for the enemy, especially if he is within sight and sound, are probably at their height.)*

Within seconds it seemed to me the glow in the East burst into flame as the tip of the sun rose finally above the horizon and day burst full upon us as it does in those climes.

"Now then, you two," commanded the leader of the Nubian guard. "Hold him in position while I drive in the nails."

It was clear they were practiced enough, for without a moment's hesitation they each seized a wrist in both hands and forcing my hands flat against the arms of the cross spreadeagled me so that I was on tiptoe, my feet barely touching the ground. Hardly was I in position. with the man on my left holding my hand from behind the cross spread flat against the beam and the man on my right facing me, than I felt a stinging pain as the executioner-in-chief thrust a sharp nail into the back of my left hand ready to drive it home through my palm and into the wood of the cross itself.

For that one brief unguarded moment his legs were apart and his weight on the nail piercing the back of my hand, while his other hand was drawn back with the hammer preparing to drive it home. All their attention was concentrated on the task in hand. My wrists were held by a powerful guard on each side with their leader about to hammer the first nail through my hand, but at least I saw the chance for one last defiant counter-blow.

"Spawn of a thousand pigs," I hissed and at the same instant kicked him with all my might between the legs.

At my words he hesitated for a fatal second before my ankle caught him with all my power behind it full in the groin. As he doubled forward in agony, the hammer blow came down hard on the wrist of the guard holding my hand flat against the wood. I heard the bone crack and his grip loosened instantly, their gasps of pain sounding as one. Tearing my arm from his weakened hold, I felt the nail fly free as I reached for the hilt of the chief executioner's scimitar now protruding invitingly towards me as he bent forward hugging his groin. Despite the pain I felt in my hand I wrenched the weapon out of his waistband and swung it forward with all the strength I possessed at the exposed neck of the guard with his back towards me still holding my right hand. The heavy blade sharpened to a razor's edge sliced through muscle, bone and gristle effortlessly, severing the vertebrae cleanly so that one second his head was on his shoulders and the next it was a black ball spouting gore and bowling down the slope between the legs of the snorting stallion.

"Here's one for Gleneil!" I found myself shouting insanely.

Then switching the scimitar to my unhurt right hand now free again, although I have always been as good with the one as the other, I swung a blow at the back of the chief executioner's head still bent forward invitingly. In the instant a second black ball spouting gore was rolling under the hooves of the now frantically rearing stallion and I could not avoid a fleeting moment's admiration for the balance and keenness of these Saracen weapons. Pausing only for a quick slash at the face of the remaining Nubian guard and seeing him fall back, I took three running strides and leaped on the back of the plunging stallion, which thre young Caliph Haroun el Fahid was trying to control. Before he even knew what was happening my left arm was round his body binding his arms to his sides and I was as firmly seated behind him as a mating toad.

"Now ride for your life, or I cut your throat," I cried in his own language, clapping my heels vigorously into the stallion's flanks and slapping its hindquarters with the flat of the bloody scimitar.

With a mighty plunge the stallion shot forward towards the Christian lines, as if propelled by a thunderbolt, and neither of us could have stopped him even had we tried. It was only the mighty trenches dug by the besieging Crusaders' army on the plain before the walls of Acre that halted his headlong gallop by which time we were amongst friends. There were plenty of friendly hands to hold the plunging stallion and help me and my captive to dismount.

My captive, the young Caliph, whose name was Haroun el Fahid, surrendered himself formally to me with some speed when he saw the threatening swords of those who crowded round us. I had some difficulty in explaining who I was to the mixed crowd of men at arms now gathered round us, but eventually I was led through the Crusaders' camp amidst a surging cheering crowd into the presence of my father. There too was Lord Dewrie, who, I was shocked to see, was lying on a stretcher, yellow and sweating, shaking with fever, his head swathed in bandages, hardly recognisable as his normal cheerful ruddy self, When I had finally explained the events of the past few days and the presence of my prisoner to them, hampered the while by their numerous questions and interruptions, my father turned to Lord Dewrie.

"You must surely agree that this day you have lost a squire and we have gained a new Knight, is that not so?"

So it was that clad only in a pair of ragged pantaloons, blood-stained and with the stink of the cell still strong about me, but with a silken cloak draped hastily about my shoulders I knelt before my father and was knighted in the privacy of his tent with my Lord Dewrie and my prisoner the Caliph Haroun el Fahid as witnesses. After this interview had been concluded I was allowed the pleasure of soaking my soiled and somewhat exhausted body in warm water and oils with Alan in attendance full of endless questions. He soon saw, however, that what I most wanted was rest and refreshment. After seeing my needs were supplied, he left me to sleep, which I did the clock round, waking the next day almost myself again.

Apart from the minor wound in the back of my left hand and a still sore head the worst I had suffered was some bruising from the shackles in which I had spent the night suspended. The most lasting thing to me was the stench of that cell itself. Even after I had washed myself with scented water and oils I felt I still had the stink of that cell in my nostrils. That and the smell of fresh cedar wood will stay with me until my dying day, for I have not often had much closer calls with death itself.

Chapter 6

Mortal Combat

The sound of the landslide I had caused, which had engulfed so many of the Nubian Guard, had been sufficient, as I had thought at the time, to warn the the Crusaders' camp of the imminent danger of attack. In fact the Guards had been so demoralised by the effects of the rockslide that they had not attempted to press home an attack but had withdrawn with the injured and the dead who had not been totally buried. The Crusaders under arms at the Tourney had barely even been aware of their danger until a force sent out to investigate had discovered the site where the vultures were feeding on the corpses of the dead protruding from the rocks. Alan was amongst those who had seen it, and said that it was a particularly grisly sight.

It transpired, however, that the whole venture, the Tourney and the Crusaders' camp in the desert, had been part of a plan prepared by King Richard and the leaders of the various forces to lure the Saracens out from the safety of the castle Acre and bring them to battle. The possibility of a surprise attack had not been overlooked, and our leaders had, in some degree been prepared for just such a sortie as had been planned, although the dawn advance through the Wadi had not been detected and could have been at least in part successful. Our Lord Dewrie was one of those privy to this plan and hence his keenness to prepare himself and us for the event, although we had not at the time been aware of the reason for his exceptional preparations. It was conceded, however, that my intervention had been instrumental in saving many lives in the battle that would undoubtedly have taken place but for the havoc I had caused to the Saracen forces in the Wadi.

Naturally enough, as I had always assumed he would, Mo-my face Alan burst into roars of laughter. After the moment or two it took for the news to sink in I too started to laugh until both of us were bent double.

"Mind you, if Father Benedict ever learns the truth you won't be laughing so loudly," Alan remarked more soberly at last.

"Like a fool I left the bellrope hanging in the middle of the chapel," I confessed. "But if we just keep quiet I don't see how he will ever know what really happened. Let James claim he saw an angel if he wishes."

"Father Benedict also found a flask of wine, a loaf of bread and half a ham behind the altar." Alan added gleefully. "It looks as if James didn't intend to go hungry or thirsty through his night's vigil. I've heard of it being done before, but never of anyone being caught out like that."

"Ah, so that's what he was doing," I exclaimed. "I saw him moving behind the altar, but I couldn't make out who it was, let alone what he was doing. Then I thought I heard him leave."

"Which was when his angel flew over the altar," exclaimed Alan, with a broad grin.

The affair caused a considerable stir for the next few days, and there were those who claimed that James Macdonnel had witnessed a miraculous visitation. There were others, more sceptical. who talked of draughts blowing out candles and of white owls in old buildings. There were also quite a number of my contemporaries who had witnessed my feats on the bellrope and either knew or guessed the truth. They must also have chattered a good deal too freely for Jamie Douglas, with an ever open ear for gossip learned of it. He made the most of it, turning the whole event into comic verse so that very soon everyone was laughing about it, and the newly knighted James Macdonnel was heard to swear vengeance on me before departing for his northern home. Father Benedict also, for a brief while, made a point of finding some of the more tiresome tasks for me to perform, but apart from that I thought the matter finished. In his absence I completely failed to realise the depths of hatred James now nourished against me.

Chapter 4

As a Squire to the Crusade

As we approached the end of our time as pages to the court and our approaching manhood became more obvious there came what was irreverently known amongst us as the 'graduation service.' Margaret de Brus, or Auld Meg, our nominal guardian, had been a noted courtesan in her day and she had not lost her interest in certain aspects of her charges. Each of us in turn would be sent up to 'warm her bed' for her. Those who pleasured her well could find themselves required for such duties on several nights in a row, for, as she herself said, there was many a fine melody could be played on an old harp. For most of us, however, while undoubtedly broadening our experience and serving as a useful foretaste of life, this was the nearest we ever came to being harpists.

It was not so very much later, towards the end of the year 1189, when I had finally progressed from being a lowly page and had attained the heights of squiredom, that the news came that the King, my father, had allied with King Richard of England to join a Third Holy Crusade against the forces of the Saracens in the East. Saladin, the great Saracen leader, we were told had defeated a body of Knights Templar and Hospitallers at Tiberius, and then conquered the whole of Palestine, including the Kingdom of Jerusalem. Only the port of Tyre remained in Christian hands. (*In the course of a masterly campaign Saladin had totally routed the Christian occupying forces, which, in view of Gleneil's comments on them when he reached Palestine, is perhaps not altogether surprising. Saladin's failure to secure the port of Tyre was an inexplicable strategic error on his part which allowed the Crusading relieving forces with their control of the sea a base from which to attack him This was an advantage of which they soon availed themselves.*)

As I learned later it was in part at least, in return for the King, my father's promise to raise a Scots army to accompany him on the Crusade that King Richard agreed to the payment of 15,000 merks to release him from the shameful bond of fealty extracted from him by Henry II at Falaise, after his capture at Berwick. There was not much doubt Richard had every intention of renouncing that agreement at a later date when it suited him. That was very much his way with any agreement. He was more a Frank by nature than English, and well used to double-dealing. Any agreements he made were always highly suspect hence why he was better known by many as Richard Yea and Nay. Instead of Coeur de Lion they would have done well to have named him Coeur de Liar.

(This is an interesting contemporary, if possibly slightly cynical, sidelight on the character of King Richard, which fits in well with the facts and with modern historical research, even if it does not match the traditional romantic picture of the chivalrous king. As third son of Henry II by Eleanor of Aquitaine, Richard had spent most of his life in France, imposing an iron rule in Aquitaine. He quarrelled with his older brother, Henry, who invaded Aquitaine and who died in the course of their minor fratricidal war. Richard then succeeded to the English throne on his father's death in 1189 whereupon he announced his intention of opposing Saladin. To raise an army of around 4,000 men at arms and 4,000 foot transported in a fleet of 100 ships for the Crusade Richard raised money recklessly by any means available clearly with very little intention, or even the possibility, of fulfilling many of the promises he made at the time. Gleneil's sometimes cynical attitude towards the Knightly code may well have been caused by him seeing at first hand Richard's blatant flouting of it, as and when it suited him. There is nothing like seeing the behaviour of the great and powerful from the inside to foster cynicism. On the other hand Gleneil did admit that Richard was a good general; see below.)

The news of the Crusade set us squires burnishing our Knight's shields and armour and putting ever finer edges on their swords and spears. We also spent hours with bow and arrow, or sword and shield, practising the arts of war. There was also the daily business of exercising our master's horses and practicing the art of tilting, aiming at the loop hanging on the cord or the quintain with its moving arm and avoiding receiving a round buffet from it, when we hit the target with the lance. (*Practising tilting was usually conducted by aiming at a metal loop suspended from a cord, or else aiming at the quintain. This was a metal figure pivoting on a central pole with a long arm at one side. When the figure was not hit cleanly it pivoted round and the arm would catch the unwary tilter a blow unless he managed to duck to avoid it. Practise at the tilting yard, of course, was not only good training for the rider but good schooling for the horse.*)

Apart from mastering the use of a lance on horseback, we squires also had to learn the art of fighting on horseback, or on foot, with the two handed broad sword, with the battle axe, the mace and with the formidable morning-star, the spiked ball and chain favoured by many knights. All these weapons, of course, had to be kept in perfect condition ready for action, The moving parts of the suits of armour also had to be polished and oiled to make for easy movement and the fitting checked for comfort and signs of wear. For the majority of squires it was a lengthy process and as their master's butts for the most part they received most of the knocks and few thanks.

One of the worst features, as I always saw it, of being a squire, was trying on the Knight's suit of armour and testing it after oiling and greasing the joints. Since most knights were very different in size from their squires it was usually an uncomfortable business at best and probably not strictly necessary, but still more effective than just testing the movement of each piece by hand. There was always a certain amount of adjustment which could be taken up on the straps which held the various pieces together, but each suit of armour was, rightly, intended to fit the man for whom it had been measured and testing the joints of ill-fitting armour was at best a painful process. Furthermore, despite one's best efforts to remove all traces of oil and grease from the joints, there were always places one had missed and after putting on the armour laboriously and checking it for freedom of movement one emerged streaked with oil and grease in every imaginable part of one's anatomy. Any tunic regularly worn under armour inevitably became stained with grease and rust as a result.

Admittedly a tunic worn under chain mail always became strongly marked with rust stains in time too, but the tunics worn under armour usually also stank strongly of sweat and oil. Perhaps that is why I personally preferred to fight in chain mail whenever possible. It really gave almost as much protection and more importantly in my view it allowed a great deal more freedom and quickness of movement. (*There seems to be an interesting parallel here between heavy tanks and light tanks or armoured cars. The really heavy tanks which moved at a ponderous top speed of something like twenty miles an hour were heavy in every sense of the word and slow to manoeuvre. The light tanks and armoured cars which could move at forty miles an hour or more were a pleasure by comparison. Anyone who has ever fought in tanks or armoured cars would agree with Gleneil's point that speed and mobility were more important than sheer weight of protective armour. The latter after all has always merely given an illusion of protection since even the heaviest armour may be pierced by a suitable weapon designed for the purpose. This must have been just as true of the Knight in armour as of the tank or armoured car and in addition wearing very heavy armour cannot have been a pleasant experience for the wearer. Nor can it have been very enjoyable being subjected to an attack by Greek Fire. cf. below.*)

After any jousting tournament, or tourney, there were almost invariably dents to be hammered out in any suit of armour. This again was usually part of the squire's duties, unless it was a job for the blacksmith. There was also the tiresome chore of polishing any silver or gold inlays, which could be a very time consuming business. All in all the task of keeping their knight's suits of armour in order was generally considered amongst the worst of any squire's duties. I certainly regarded it as such.

Alan and I, however, were fortunate in that we were together and the knight we both served was the Earl of Dewrie, a cousin of the King, my father, and hence indirectly a kinsman. As he was highly placed in court circles we had the advantage of being amongst the first to hear at first hand any news of important matters, although this was usually only confirmation of court gossip already freely circulating in the servants quarters. In theory we should also have had to work doubly hard to ensure that his horses, arms and armour were always in first class condition and ready for service. Fortunately as a man of considerable fortune, thanks to the ransom his father, the first Earl, had received nearly forty years previously for a Saracen nobleman captured in the 2nd Crusade in 1148, he was able to employ his own master-at-arms, and was accompanied by his own troop of archers and spearmen, as well as sufficient grooms and lackeys to make our work comparatively easy and mainly a matter of supervision rather than extremely hard labour, as it might well have been otherwise. Instead of being constantly black with oil, grease and sweat we were able for the most part to supervise others doing the hard work, while we practised tilting at the quintain or vied with each other in mock combat.

The master-at-arms was a thick set dark Lowland Scot named John Weir, who had served the Dewrie family for many years and whom we soon found we could rely on for any advice on matters concerned with the running of the household and the men-at-arms In short, although kept busy enough in all conscience, our tasks were not as onerous as those of many squires with less wealthy masters, for apart from supervising the care of his arms, armour and horses, it consisted mainly in attending my lord when he was hunting, hawking and fowling or dining and roistering. These last two duties were not as easy as they might sound for the Lord De-wrie, though appearing at first sight somewhat portly was well muscled and lusty enough, enjoyed wining, wenching and gaming to the full, and it was a hard task at times to keep up with his excesses without ending up with a sore head or the pox.

On the other hand, it was seldom necessary to be on call again bright and early the next day, for it would usually be midday before my lord was calling for possets and unguents for his aching head, or else demanding his horse and his hounds preparatory to working off his excesses with some hard exercise. Even so this was often a test of our own reserves of strength and patience. In its way it was an interesting if sometimes hectic introduction to a life we had hitherto only observed at second hand.

By this time I was a fit and sinewy seventeen year old, perhaps on the lean side, certainly not over large with puppy fat. I was lithe and quick on my feet and able to fell a man twice my weight and size, thanks to the training of Jamie Douglas. I was also able to withstand cold and ride or run for long distances after hounds, or in chain mail, thanks to the training of my old mentors at Beaulieu and their successors in Edinburgh. In addition I was a competent performer with most weapons, including the lance after years of practise at the quintain, and I had an innate aptitude with horses and hounds. Filled with youthful enthusiasm to put my fighting skills to the test I was naturally enough eager to set off for the Holy land and my first taste of war against the Saracens. Both Alan and I, old friends and rivals, were much of a size and age, eager to serve our master in every way, and he in his turn seemed well pleased with us.

(*Squires appear to have been very much in the position of newly promoted second lieutenants, exercising a mild authority in theory, but in reality little more than figureheads learning their job. The Master-at-arms seems to have been more in the nature of the Regimental Sergeant major who was at the centre of matters and really in control of affairs. It also sounds as if squires to ordinary knights had a somewhat tougher time of it than those to wealthy and well-connected knights. This sounds rather like the difference between subalterns in run-of-the-mill infantry or armoured regiments and those in select Guards or Cavalry regiments. While few ordinary second lieutenants would have been privileged to carouse regularly with their senior officers, there could well have been exceptions in some of the more exclusive Guards or Cavalry regiments, especially for the subaltern with close royal connections. even if on the wrong side of the blanket. Life in the upper echelons of military or court circles may not really have changed all that much . . . until recently, of course!*)

This was a year of endless rumour and counter rumour. Firm news as to the date of our departure for the Holy Land arrived almost daily and as frequently was followed by another postponement. So the weeks, and then the months, dragged on until the Spring of 1190, a full year since the first news of the Crusade had reached us, when we finally received marching orders. Then everything suddenly seemed to happen with a rush. With the king, my father, we made a tour of

Perth and Stirling, then the Border marches, gathering ever more forces on the way, and ending at the old town of Berwick in the Merse with its powerful castle below Halidon Hill overlooking the river Tweed. The King, my father, and his entire court spent two nights feasting here which must have impoverished the knight commander considerably.

(King William, of course, had been captured here by the English and no doubt had bitter memories of it. He would probably have approved of its modern transformation. The castle ruins were totally demolished in the 19th century and it is now the site of Berwick railway station, with a handsome arched railway bridge crossing the Tweed. Gleneil does not say where the bulk of the forces accompanying the king were encamped. Probably they were mostly camped on Halidon Hill above the castle, or else billetted in Berwick itself. In any army the commanding officers generally manage to fare well enough, but it can be a different story for the rank and file. On the other hand a mediaeval army such as this must have been a somewhat amorphous body moving over the country rather like a swarm of locusts living off the land as they went, leaving a trail of plundered and angry countrymen behind them. Even where the aim was a Christian one, and officially approved by all, there must have been considerable local resentment as the Crusading army, or its followers, spoiled crops, killed livestock or burned woods as they passed.)

From there the army marched to Leith where a fleet had been assembled to transport us to France. The Scots army, knights, men-at-arms and camp followers, grooms, lackeys, wives, cooks and scullions, amounted to an impressive array, making a column several miles in length, marshalled around Edinburgh and the port of Leith. Getting them on board ship was a lengthy process.

This was my first experience of transporting horses by sea, although I had experience enough of sailing in fishing boats at Beaulieu as a lad. The fleet itself was a motley selection ranging from large foreign-looking carvel-built broad-beamed and high-pooped vessels with one or even two banks of oars as well as two masts, to narrower clinker built coastal cargo carriers with a single mast and just a few oarsmen and crew, such as were commonly to be found in the northern waters. The bulk of Earl Dewrie's forces were embarked successfully enough onto a large French built two-masted boat La Margaruite that had sailed from Calais, which was to be our destination.

Once we had cleared the mouth of the Firth of Forth, it was a stirring sight to see so many vessels together at one time. We had only been at sea for a day and a half, however, and were not far beyond Berwick, when an unexpected storm blew up and the fleet was soon scattered. The majority of the men at arms and camp followers were soon laid low with seasickness, while those of us who were fit enough toiled at the oars or in bucket chains baling out the endless seawater to prevent us being capsized or sinking. Even so we shipped several waves which nearly sank us and despite our best efforts washed overboard some of the deck cargo stored in the forepart of the ship including four of the horses. Fortunately the storm blew itself out in the end, after a frightening twenty four hours without more damage than a few leaks in the planking. Even so it was a full ten days before we made our landfall at Calais, and we were all mightily relieved to disembark safely. The horses especially had suffered badly from lack of food and attention during the storm and from being confined tightly in partitions on the main deck. My Lord Dewrie's charger, a grey, named Remus, and my own bay stallion, Beau, whom I had attended personally, were well enough considering their ordeal.

It was in the course of this voyage that I became good friends with John Weir, the Master-at-Arms. Hitherto he had always been somewhat withdrawn, understandably perhaps, keeping himself deliberately at a distance from the two new raw young squires, ostensibly his superiors although lacking his very considerable experience. On the first day at sea even while suffering the worst pangs of seasickness he had stood smartly at attention with his weapons freshly burnished in spite of the salt spray and his men drawn up smartly in line for inspection. I had returned his smart salute and then he had bent double in a paroxysm of sickness and spewed his guts out over the deck between us. I dismissed him to his quarters to sleep it off and then a few short hours afterwards was toiling by his side as we all, landsmen and crew alike, took our turns at the oars, or did our best to bale out the water below decks. In one particularly stormy period as we crossed the deck together to take our place at the oars a wave swept him off his feet and had I not managed to grasp his sleeve he could well have been washed overboard. It was a trivial enough happening, but he seemed to feel he owed me his life, Such events do indeed draw men together, and I in my turn had to admire his refusal to admit defeat even at the hand of that worst of scourges, seasickness, from which fortunately I have never suffered.

Despite our losses we had fared better than many others, for it was a full week longer before the last of the fleet had limped into Calais and some of the vessels were reported sunk or wrecked. It was another week before our forces were deemed sufficiently recovered to continue on our way. Meanwhile we had been re-inforced by a force of Normans under a Count de Lusignan a relative of the notorious Guy de Lusignan, one of King Richard's favourites, who later was to be designated somewhat prematurely King of Jerusalem, then afterwards King of Cyprus. Together, under the sign of the Cross, we set off southwards on our journey to the east.

The journey through France seemed unending. The dust and monotony of each day's march was only enlivened by an occasional day's hunting for deer or boar, when signs of either were discovered. On the whole the inhabitants of the countryside were indifferent to our arrival. The sign of the Cross which we wore was sufficient to show our peaceful intent, but already in the previous year other Crusading forces had passed and any zeal they may have felt for the Cause was a thing of the past. They may have fed and feted the first Crusaders to pass their way, but for the most part we had to pay our way or else our men and horses would have starved. As it was we arrived at Toulon, our port of departure on the coast off the Ligurian sea, dark as blackamoors from the sun and a good deal leaner and more experienced than when we had left Scotland. Already we fancied ourselves seasoned warriors, although for the most part we had no idea of what was in prospect.

It seemed a considerable fleet had been waiting our arrival for close on a month and once again we had the tiresome business of loading horses and men aboard ship. The ship on which we embarked was markedly different from that on which we had journeyed to France from Leith. It was much longer and narrower, although it too had two masts and a single bank of oars. The captain was a Moor with a sword slash across his jaw, which made his speech difficult to understand, but that apart he seemed to have his ship and his crew under good control. It may also have been that we too had learned some discipline, but in any event we managed to settle down for the voyage quickly enough.

Hugging the coastline of Italy on the edge of the Tyrrhenian sea we passed between the Isle of Sicily and the toe of Italy through the Strait of Messina into the great Mediterranean sea. Here we encountered a storm which blew for nearly a week and took us before it past the Isle of Crete with the sails furled and all hands taking turns at the oars. When the storm finally had worn itself out, the sun came out and we were soon experiencing for the first time the heat of the eastern climes. Becalmed now, with no wind, we again had to take our turns at the oars and in that heat it was hard work. Then it turned out the water barrels had been damaged in the gale.

"The captain says we must make port at Episcopi in Cyprus to take on water and provisions. And I for one will be glad to get ashore," Alan added as he told me the news.

It was another two days before we came in sight of Mount Olympus, towering over the island of Cyprus. Even then our progress seemed painfully slow, but fortunately, with the remains of our fresh water all but exhausted, a favourable wind started to blow. In a few hours we were alongside the quay in the harbour of the small port of Episcopi, where the white houses by the quayside reflected the sun with dazzling intensity which almost hurt the eyes.

This was our opportunity to take on provisions as well as fresh water and the chance to stretch our legs was welcome enough. The people who greeted us on the quayside were for the most part surly Moors, mainly fisherfolk as far as we could make out. However we were told that the pine clad slopes of Mount Olympus dominating the background also contained copper mines, which apparently was the islanders' main source of wealth. While the crew aided by the men at arms were replenishing our water, Alan and I were sent to purchase fresh fruit, oranges, lemons and melons and some meat in the form of chickens and goats in the local market place. In this small but very busy market place, surrounded by a square of dazzling white houses reflecting the sun, we spent some time trying to make ourselves understood at various stalls in a mixture of languages and all the while fending off various importunate beggars.

We had almost lost patience when we were approached by a fat Moorish figure in flowing robes, who thrust aside all the others gathered round us. He bowed to us graciously and greeted us in heavily accented but reasonably fluent Latin.

"A thousand welcomes to you, honourable sirs," he began. "May I, Mohammed, humble master of the bazaar in Tyre, make myself known to you. If I can be of any assistance to you please let your wishes be known and it will be my pleasure to assist you in any way I can."

"We are looking for provisions for our ship, Mohammed," explained Alan.

"Please call me Mo!" he replied immediately with an ingratiating display of gleaming teeth. "Just tell me what you wish and it shall be your's at a very reasonable price."

It was very quickly apparent that he had the measure of the local traders. We soon realised that we would be returning to our vessel with the choicest fruits and plumpest beasts that were available having paid a good deal less than we would almost certainly have had to pay without his help. It was then that a thought occurred to me

"I would like you to find me a servant, who could help me learn your local tongues," I suggested. "I need someone with a wide command of languages."

"Your every wish is my command," he replied immediately. "There is a visiting slavemaster here, called Hussein, who should be able to help you. He has a great many slaves and is bound to have one to suit your needs. He is totally untrustworthy, but I will deal with him for you."

He spoke briefly to a large fat man with a black moustache standing in the background who came forward smiling ingratiatingly.

"I, Saddam Hussein, know a very fine young man who will suit you intimately," he said at once in oily tones. "Very choice. Very healthy. And very obedient. All my slaves are very obedient and I am slavemaster over a very large region."

"All I want is someone who will be able to correct my grammar and teach me the various languages," I replied firmly.

"Absolutely," he beamed. "It shall be as you wish. I have a very fine young man in mind for you. He has been my own personal servant but still a virgin. Very clean and very loving. A bottom like a perfect peach. For thirty silver groats he is yours. A splendid Christian bargain as you might say. I will send him to you."

Without waiting for my reply the slavemaster siezed Mohammed's sleeve and led him away into one of the houses fronting the market place. A few moments later I was pleasantly surprised when a light skinned young Saracen urchin came out and showed his white teeth in a beaming smile.

"My name is Hassan. Mohammed el Phayeed, descendant of all the Pharoahs, has told my master Hussein to send me to you," he announced importantly in passable Latin. "I have come to be your personal servant."

"Hmmph. Tricky fellows those Pharoahs I seem to recall," remarked Alan dubiously. "I don't like the sound of that."

"My grandfather was a Norman knight in the Second Crusade," the lad continued. "And I can speak many tongues, for I have travelled from the lands of Solomon in the far off desert and have served in the courts of Saladin himself. Your every wish is my command."

He then proved his point by chattering away in several tongues, most of which I could not understand. It struck me at once that Alan and I would find him a useful lad, handy for running errands and as a personal servant. In spite of Alan's doubts I decided to take him. In fact we soon found him invaluable in many ways as well as reasonably honest and in my case a good tutor in the languages most commonly encountered in the market places. His artless chatter was difficult to follow at first, but I soon found him a useful source of local gossip and a reliable barometer of native opinions.

(After any war there are always children left behind fathered by the forces of both sides. This must have been true after the Second Crusade and previous wars just as it was of the Third Crusade and subsequent wars in the region; many soldiers also remained behind and settled down with local girls. Any well fought over area invariably has a somewhat mongrel population as a result of such matings and the Middle East in particular must have been greatly affected in this way. This can be a permanent cause of internal dissensions and cannot be ignored as one of the many contributory factors which have hindered the region's prospects for achieving a lasting peace over the centuries.)

We had hardly decided to employ the lad when the portly grey haired merchant, Mohammed, and the oily slavemaster appeared once more. The slavemaster accepted the purchase price with alacrity and promptly disappeared. Mohammed, the portly merchant, remained with us. He obviously knew or had guessed that we were headed for Tyre, since that was the only port available to the Crusaders on the coast of Palestine at the time. and he was not long in coming to the point.

"Would it be possible for me to take passage with you, honourable sirs?" he asked. "I am sure that at times the very Gods conspire against me. My own vessel in which I arrived a week past has sprung a leak, and it will be a month before it is seaworthy. Yet it is urgent I return to my home in Tyre. It will give me great pleasure to serve you in any way I can. I have a great admiration for the Knights of Normandy, also the Frankish Knights and those of England."

"We're Scots," replied Alan sharply.

"I have an even greater admiration for the Knights of the land of the Scots," he replied with a fine display of his gleaming teeth, and we could neither of us help smiling in return at his obvious determination to please at all costs.

"I have considerable influence in Tyre," he added. "Anything that you desire there it will be my pleasure to provide. As Hassan will tell you I am well known there."

"We will see what we can do," Alan promised him as we left the market place.

After we had returned to the ship and referred the matter to my

Lord Dewrie, it was decided to take him on as dragoman, or guide and general interpreter. While Alan went back to the market place to inform him he that he could join us as our dragoman, I attended to having the fresh fruit and beasts brought on board the ship with the ready help of Hassan. Hearing a commotion going on I glanced round in time to see Alan chasing the fat merchant up the quayside directly towards me. The man was looking back at Alan in alarm and not really looking where he was going. With only a few yards to go he looked up, saw me and, attempting to avoid me, tripped and fell flat like a tent collapsing.

"Mercy, masters, mercy! Indeed the Gods conspire against me yet again!" he gasped, as Alan came up beside him. "I am sorry if I have offended you, but please say that I may accompany you."

"Oh, yes. All right, you may," replied Alan. "But get up and don't ever make a mistake like that again with us."

As the fat merchant picked himself up and sidled away followed by the laughter and ribald comments of a number of the crew who had watched from the deck, I caught a murderous look in his eye. Nevertheless his voice and manner remained respectful as, head averted, he gabbled out his thanks and made good his escape.

"What was that all about?" I asked curiously.

"When I told him my Lord Dewrie had agreed to him accompanying us he thanked me profusely for using my influence, and handed me a flat brown canvas wallet," explained Alan, still with a trace of indignation in his voice. "Inside were ten gold pieces. The fellow was trying to pay me."

"What did you do?" I asked with a smile

"I threw it at his head," answered Alan with an answering grin. "Then I think he thought I was going to attack him, which I must admit had occurred to me, and he set off like a greyhound. I was surprised how fast he he could move for his size too. And all the while he kept saying that every Eastern squire and knight and all the Norman, Frankish and English Knights he had ever known had been delighted to accept a reward for their services, and it was customary to provide it. So I told him that wasn't how we behaved, and he had better learn that right now."

The corpulent merchant soon returned to join the ship and seemed outwardly to bear no ill feelings for his public humiliation, though once or twice when he thought we were not looking, I suspected I had caught a sidelong glance of brooding malice towards Alan and myself. It was quickly very obvious that behind the almost always smiling exterior there was a devious and calculating mind. His unctuous servility too was more assumed than real and he liked to know everything that was going on. He soon appeared to know intimate details about everyone on board our ship from the Captain down to the lowest members of the crew. He in turn soon became known for his frequent assertion that the Gods, or some specific individuals, were conspiring against him. Yet there were few details of our life on board ship which he failed to note.

It did not for instance escape his notice that my occasional conversations in the kitchens at the court in Edinburgh with the Saracen cook and the Nubian scullions had not been wasted. Despite the many different dialects and accents amongst the crew on board the ship I was usually able to gather at least an idea of what was being said. With the knowledge of various useful phrases and words I had picked up in Edinburgh I found I could also generally make myself understood without too much difficulty. I had at least a useful grounding on which to work, and I very quickly found the boy Hassan a helpful tutor.

As we were preparing to enter his home port of Tyre, Mohammed Phayeed took the opportunity of approaching me with his ingratiating beaming smile, exposing that row of gleaming teeth.

"Greetings honoured sir. It is unusual for a Frank to speak the Saracen tongue," he remarked. "Where did you learn to speak our tongue so well."

"I am a Scot, not a Frank, as you have been told before," I replied, patiently. "I knew certain Saracen captives in our land, and it was from them I learned all I know of your language. I am still far from fluent."

"Nay. Not so," he replied, with an air of what appeared to be genuine surprise. "It seems to me that you need little more to be mistaken for a native of Tyre. You have the accent and intonation to the manner born. A month or so and no-one would know the difference."

He was, however, very much a man with an eye to the main chance. He was for ever paying extravagant compliments, praising anyone he considered might be of use to him at some future date, so I paid little attention to him at the time, beyond naturally feeling mildly flattered, as he had intended. I was more interested in the harbour we were approaching. It was on the inland side of what I later learned was the narrow island of Tyre, lying just off the coast. The sparkling white buildings shining brilliantly in the shimmering sunlight were tall and impressive. As we approached nearer we could see the harbour full of vessels and the quaysides thronged with a crush of onlookers.

As we prepared to make fast alongside the quay the value of Mohammed el Phayeed became at once apparent. The fat and always smiling dragoman suddenly began to spit out commands to various individuals on the quayside in tones which brooked no refusal in any language. It was clear that he was known and feared by most of those he addressed. Our mooring ropes were speedily secured to bollards on the quayside and the numerous vendors touting their wares suddenly withdrew to a reasonable distance and while it was too much to expect them to cease their cajoling, at least they did not press on us quite so importunately.

"It appears that your fat friend is a person of some consequence," remarked Lord Dewrie approvingly to Alan and myself. "We seem to have done well to bring him with us."

In fact we soon found that this was the case, at least as far as our arrival was concerned. Any supplies we required were at once available. Nor were we forced to indulge in endless haggling before a price could be agreed. His boast that he controlled the bazaar in Tyre seemed indeed to be close to the truth. This was unusual, for the majority of Moors we encountered, and certainly those of the lower orders, were not only arrant thieves, not to be trusted with anything moveable, but also inveterate liars as well. With most merchants such as Phayeed, who had attained a certain standing, one could be reasonably sure that sooner or later they would demand a return for services provided which far outweighed any benefit provided. Rather to our surprise, however, soon after supervising the unloading of our vessel he took his withdrawal after assuring us yet again of his assistance whenever we required it. He himself, it transpired, had an imposing residence amongst the tall buildings of Tyre, while we were encamped inland near to the source of the springs which supplied the harbour with its ample water supply.

Another dragoman was assigned to us in his place, a fat Frank with a Moorish look about him, who, in the manner of the rest of them, at once informed us that he could fulfill our every wish, but whom we equally soon found to be an arrant rogue, incapable of telling the truth when a lie would suffice. In appearance not unlike Mohammed el Phayeed, to whom he claimed to be related, although the name, or its many variants, was apparently as common as John Smith, we found the man to be as typical of his kind as could be. (*It is interesting to note that a clan of Scottish gypsies or tinkers named Faa, or possibly Phaa, claiming to be of Egyptian origin' were well known throughout Scotland during the 18th and 19th centuries having their base deep in the Borders at Yetholm*).

Whether of Moorish or Frankish origins, these dragomen were a special species of rogue, always claiming to be helpful to any new arrivals, but scarcely more than outright thieves, offering to provide any service or fulfill any need and lining their pockets by charging exorbitant prices. This fat rogue was not only an open and outrageous thief but also the father of all liars. He had a stall in the local bazaar which sold almost everything imaginable, much of it quite useless and almost all of it stolen. The Moors were almost to a man blatant thieves and we soon found that if anything was left unguarded for a moment it almost immediately vanished as if by magic. We also quickly discovered that if anything was stolen from our camp within a few hours we could almost certainly buy its exact likeness at a bargain price from his or his brother's stall in the bazaar. (*Very little seems to have changed today in this respect at least. It was an accepted fact of life in some areas of the Middle East during the 1939–45 war that if you were unwise enough to leave your transport unguarded and you found the wheels missing from your Jeep on your return you could always purchase them back at the local bazaar.*

In that Mohammed el Phayeed had overall control of the bazaar and the stallholders, charging them, so they claimed. exorbitant rates, he was, of course, really the biggest thief of all and I was reminded of one of Jamie Douglas's lectures on the subject.

"There's aye someone wi' his hand in other people's pouches. But once theft gets big enough as like as not it then becomes respectable. It's aye a question of size. The bigger the merchant you might say the bigger the thief. They may drive the money lenders out of the temple but the high priest will still get his share from someone. On the other hand the man who lends money to the King is likely to become an Earl, or else find his head missing from his neck. Either way he'll likely not get his money back. It's a kind of chancy business yon. Much like horse thieving, I'd say, but maybe not just as honest. It's aye the same, however, in all walks o' life, the higher a man climbs the further he has to fall, thieves and honest men alike. The difference is the thief will likely have a rope round his neck. That's the only thought keeps many a man on the straight and narrow. And it aye makes him mighty righteous when someone else is caught out and it isn'a him. But there's aye someone with his hand in other people's pouches."

It was a strange feeling once on shore to realise that at last we had reached Palestine, the Holy Land, the land we had heard so much about from the priests and from our studies, in my case all too perfunctory, of the Bible. My first impressions were of dirt, sand and dust and flies, above all of flies. They seemed to be everywhere, settling in clouds around one's head. It was almost essential to carry a whisk made of palmleaves or horse hair to keep them at bay, though we soon found the juice of the walnut a useful deterrent. The sand too was almost as bad. It seemed to get everywhere, into one's hair, clothes, and food and even the water tasted gritty.

Then there was the special smell and feel of the place, so difficult to describe yet striking one immediately on setting foot ashore and quite unique. It was a compelling compound of heated air, strong odours of animals and men, of ordure and a strange underlying musky scent of the land itself, On one's immediate arrival on the quayside it was the first thing that assailed and overwhelmed the senses, but, like the sand and the flies, one quickly became acclimatised to it and after a short while one barely became conscious of it at all. Yet, equally, I was sure it was not something one ever completely forgot, for it was the smell of the East itself.

Underfoot the soil was mostly sandy, poor stuff for growing crops, or grazing beasts. Those cattle there seemed to be lean brutes with strange shapes, and soon too we saw our first camels, ungainly beasts, with long necks, Roman noses and drooping underlips. The Moors were dark skinned dressed in gowns which covered their heads, and their women were often veiled, but with bold eyes. It all seemed very strange to us, but first we had to march our men and horses to the Crusader's encampment outside the port itself. The men were full of excitement at their first glimpse of a foreign port, and after several weeks abstinence the talk was of all the promised delights of dusky eastern maidens, of wondrous undulating belly dancers, gyrating curvaceous females performing exotic dances to strange wailing music, and the desire to check the truth of the oft repeated travellers' tales of the sexual abilities and prowess of Moorish women. I have to confess that these were subjects on which Alan and I also had some interesting discussions and arguments which we also were not long in putting to the test.

As we were amongst the earliest of the Crusading force to arrive we had the choice of a reasonable site for our tents. The Crusaders' camp was composed of rows of tents forming a haphazard township of its own with the various kings, princes and noblemen holding their own courts surrounded by their supporters. We were fortunate in that we were placed close to my father's tent at the centre of our Scottish contingent of knights and men at arms. Some way beyond us were the Franks with a separate group of Norman knights alongside them. Many of these seemed to have relatives and friends amongst the Frankish and Norman knights who had settled in the area forty years or more before after the Second Crusade. Beyond them again was a party under Leopold of Austria. Next to us was an area reserved for Richard of England's court and his larger contingent of followers, who, we were warned, were some months delayed. (*This was scarcely surprising. It was no mean logistical feat, especially in those days, raising a mixed force of around 8,000 fighting men and a fleet of 100 ships. Thus even though he may have started to plan matters in 1189 Richard inevitably took a considerable time raising the forces he wanted but he also took his time on the journey to the Holy Land, stopping off on the way to attack and conquer Cyprus. His favourite, Guy de Lusignan, was later appointed King there, after first being designated somewhat prematurely King of Jerusalem.*)

It was extremely hard at first for us newcomers to follow the divisions, intrigues and constantly changing alliances between the numerous Eastern groups on both sides. There were the Knights Templar, the Knights of Malta, the Knights of Jerusalem and many other groups of knights, mostly of Norman Frankish origins, who were all loosely bound together, but the intrigues and alliances between them were constantly changing. The Saracens, although largely united under Saladin, seemed equally divided into tribes and groups under Caliphs and other minor leaders, who from time to time were also prepared to ally themselves with one or another group amongst the Crusading forces.

Since the Second Crusade had ended, most of the Eastern Knights who had remained in the area had been living in a constant state of half warfare, half truce, with the Saracens. Proud of their Frankish or Norman origins they were quick to take offence at any imagined slight. In many ways to the untutored eye these Eastern Knights, dark skinned as many Moors, were at times almost indistinguishable from the Saracen Caliphs with whom they alternately fought or lived side by side with in uneasy intimacy. Existing thus, cheek by jowl, they were, of neccessity involved in trading and dealing with each other in times of peace and had, willy nilly, had to adjust to a similar way of life.

They seemed at first a strange mixture to us fresh from Europe. With their faces darkened by the sun, their flowing robes, silken pantaloons and scimitars they appeared more at ease with the customs of the Saracens than with those of the Franks and Normans to whom they claimed to be related. Their familiarity with the

Saracen tongue, with which they interspersed their speech, and their own often limited ability to make themselves understood made them seem as foreign to us as the Moors themselves. Many of them also seemed little more than armed merchants, who appeared to live by trading and fighting in various parts of Palestine and Syria, or even simply as outright brigands, prepared to fight anyone for a price rather than a cause and without any firm belief or religion.

We soon became aware that the Crusaders' camp was a nest of intrigue. The Franks and Normans and those English who had already arrived were at odds with each other and both seemed to expect the Scots party under my father to side with them. Then there was a strong faction amongst the Eastern Frankish knights who saw themselves as the only people who understood the situation and who, while having something in common with their Frank or Norman cousins, often felt themselves slighted by them.

It was noticeable that while there were certain similarities between them there were also deep rooted differences in attitude between many of those Eastern Knights claiming Frankish or Norman origins. Both tended to claim noble or heroic antecedents and, if one was to believe all one heard, Charlemagne must have been too busy siring progeny to have had time for much else. On the other hand, although each group appeared outwardly much the same at first sight, those claiming Norman descent were usually particularly proud of their origins and even more prone to take offence at unintentional slights. They set much stock by Saints days and celebrations when they would meet wearing their national dress, carefully set aside for such occasions, singing their cherished native songs, reciting heroic poetry and drinking toasts to their famous warriors and poets, and performing wild national dances.

It was all a somewhat strange initiation for us. Instead of making an immediate attack on the forces of Saladin it seemed there was an intermission in the fighting. The all-conquering Saladin, it appeared, had recently been besieging Tyre, but had been beaten off and had then withdrawn to Acre. A Crusading force had in turn sailed to besiege his stronghold there as soon as sufficient numbers had been marshalled together. No sooner had they arrived and encamped before the Castle of Acre than their forces in turn were surrounded, more or less cut off except for reinforcement by sea over which we had the mastery. Meanwhile it seemed that we in Tyre had little to do except get used to the dust and flies, the baking sun and the natives.

Once we were comfortably settled in our new camp and Alan and I had more or less worked out our routine each day, I made a point of visiting Mohammed el Phayeed in his town house to tell him of my satisfaction with the boy Hassan, whom I took with me. Although like most of these houses it was outwardly a seeming blank white wall, once through the outer wooden gate one found oneself ushered into a cool courtyard out of the sound and bustle of the streets outside. As the fat merchant bustled forward and bowed obsequiously, I noticed Hassan taking shelter at my side in an uncharacteristic way.

"A thousand welcomes to my humble home, honoured sir," Phayeed greeted me, with his usual gleaming smile, bowing yet again. "In what way may I be of service to you. I trust the lad Hassan has been of use to you and you have found him helpful in every way. You do not wish to send him back to me?"

It so chanced that, feeling Hassan shrinking behind me at these words. I glanced downwards and caught a mirror image of Phayeed's face reflected in a brass tray on a small table to one side. The look of pure hatred on it even distorted by the decorations on the tray came as a shock to me, although I had once or twice suspected his feelings towards Alan and myself were not as friendly as he made out. I managed to control myself and informed him rather more curtly than I had intended of my satisfaction with the boy, but I did not accept his invitation to take a cooling drink of sweet lemon. I departed fairly unceremoniously keenly aware that Alan and I had no friend in that quarter. I was conscious also that the boy Hassan shared my relief at returning to the bustle of the street outside once more.

As I had already found on the boat and as Mohammed el Phayeed had noted, my time spent in the kitchens chatting with the Saracen serving wench and the Nubian scullions in Edinburgh had not been wasted. It was not long before with the help of Hassan and my own facility for any new language I was able to make myself understood well enough in the bazaars and to understand at least the gist of most of what was being said. Truth to tell, however, there seemed an infinity of tongues, or dialects, to be heard in the streets and bazaars. There were almost as many, indeed, as there were shades of skin and religions, for this I soon found was the eastern melting pot where many different races and differing types of mankind met together.

Here were slaves from far away places across the desert with tattooed and scarred faces, black as coal, and hawk nosed men with skins light as ours, or fat sweating brown merchants like our rogue of an interpreter Phayeed, all of whom spoke quite different tongues and most of whom it seemed worshipped different Gods. Although there were basically Christians and Moslems the various forms of worship and belief amongst them seemed infinite. Then again there were the eternal divisions about religion. The interpretation of the meaning of phrases in the bible seemed to lead to constant squabbling and schisms between the various Christian factions.

There were Shi-ite and Coptic Christians, there were followers of the Pope in Constantinople and the Pope in Rome and numerous other sects who claimed their's was the one true faith. The Kurds, the Syrians, the Ottomans, and the Saracens themselves, along with Nubians and numerous other races from the depths of Solomon's empire in Africa, as well as merchant trains with attendant mounted warriors, both light skinned and dark, who had come over the mountains from further East, made up a polyglot mass, many of whom were Christians of a sort. As far as I could make out it was much the same with the Saracens, who as Moslems seemed to have a diversity of followers, quite apart from the numerous black heathens who mostly as far as I could make out worshipped different Gods of their own. It was confusing to find so many different believers in the one true God all fighting one another. (*This does not sound very different from the scene there today or in many other parts of the world.*)

I was reminded of what Jamie Douglas so often said ; "There are only two things that can make the human race fall out and always will. They are religion and power. Put two men of different religion together and they will fall out. Put two powerful men together, or two men who wish to be powerful, and they too will fall out. Both lead to intrigue and plotting and often to war. It is as well I have no strong feelings about either." He would then generally perform a series of cartwheels or handsprings to show his complete contempt for such matters. (*Jamie Douglas appears to have been an extremely talented court fool with an obvious gift for satirical comment as well as a keen eye for personal foibles and weaknesses and the ability to make his point in verse or personal converse with a humorous edge to it. Today he would probably have made a fortune as a TV personality and political interviewer. Substituting politics for power his comments apply equally well in the world today.*)

At the court in Edinburgh Jamie Douglas had noted that the lighter skinned Saracen cook and the black skinned Nubian scullions appeared to have different faiths which were very little affected by regular attempts by the priests to convert them to Christianity. Needless to say, he made one of his usual startling and thoroughly heretical comments on it, which I had not forgotten

"The Romans maybe had a point when they worshipped various Gods for different reasons and there are plenty in this court, priests included, who worship Bacchus regularly in flagons of wine. But, red or white, wine has the same effect, whether the drinker is white, black or brown, or just plain dirty, and anyway the Gods should be above such human failings as judging people by the colour of their skin. Maybe the priests should try converting the heathens with barrels of wine, but, rather than ask them what colour of wine they prefer, perhaps they should ask them what colour of God they prefer?"

Once we had settled comfortably in our tents Alan and I had soon worked out our routine each day. In common with the rest of the Crusading army one thing quickly became apparent to us and that was the impossibility of wearing the clothes to which we were accustomed in that heat. The winter months of November and December lay ahead, but we there was little sign of it in these eastern climes, with the sun shining fiercely on us each day from cloudless blue skies. Doublet and hose woven from sheep's wool were unbearably hot to wear and soon brought us out in a heat rash, although in the colder nights it was a welcome garb. Yet protection from the sun at midday was very necessary. Either a strip of cloth around the loins, or the loose baggy pantaloons of the average Saracen, or the full silken or goatskin gown which protected the wearer from the sun's rays were the normal garb, depending on status and the time of day.

Nor, we soon found, was armour ideally suited to the climate. Wearing chain mail or full armour in that sun was too painful for even the most hardened of souls. After an hour or two the sweat was pouring off the poor wight inside and the metal was too hot to touch. Furthermore any oil or grease in the joints became clogged with sand and flies and it could become difficult, if not impossible, to move freely. The armour itself also seemed to attract scorpions and other noxious creatures, so that it had to be inspected regularly. It was not a pleasant sensation to feel such unwanted visitors crawling over one's body inside a suit of armour. Lice, cockroaches and fleas were bad enough in all conscience.

"I would not condemn a man to be broiled in such a way," admitted the Earl himself. "I can see the need for a cloth covering to protect the wearer from this accursed sun."

The oiled cloaks we used at home to protect a knight in armour from rain and snow, although some protection from the sun, after an hour or so proved too heavy and hot. We were not long in learning that the Frankish Eastern Knights had their own ways of adapting to the climate. Because of what seemed to us their excessive use of light and flowing silken garments we at first mocked them with the nickname of Silken Eastern Knights. (*With an insularity natural enough in an island race, the British, especially when on service abroad, tend to find generic nicknames for foreigners. Although not an exact parallel, in the British Forces during the 1939–45 War the title Worthy Oriental Gentleman was widely applied to the subjects of King Farouk and all those whom Gleneil would have termed 'Moors.'*) However we soon found for ourselves that the use of silk or some light covering was almost a necessity in those climes, more especially when wearing armour. Although at first their ways seemed strange to us, it was soon clear that they knew how to live in very different conditions to our chill northern clime. To go bareheaded or without covering in the heat of the day we soon discovered was enough to drive a man mad, for the sun soon dulled the wits and rendered speech and even the ability to walk in a straight line well nigh impossible. For the most part we adopted something similar to that worn by the Saracens themselves. (*Sunstroke has always been a problem for any Europeans in the Middle or Far East and the solutions have been many and varied, ranging from the absurdly heavy Topee, or pith helmet, of the 19th century to the kepi of the French Foreign Legion. The Arabian headdress however has always been particularly suited to the climate and during the 1939-45 war in the desert was adopted by the Long Range Desert Group as the most sensible wear for their purposes. It seems the Crusaders, or at least the Scots amongst them, took the same view.*)

The means of transport in these parts was also something of a surprise to us. The horses were small and light boned, but spirited and strong, able to stand the climate and immensely speedy, while also able to withstand long journeys without food or water. They could, however, not begin to stand the weight of a knight in armour. Surprisingly the donkeys which were to be seen everywhere could carry enormous loads and so too could the asses, both of which, along with the oxen, were amongst the main beasts of burden. The alternative was a camel. With their massive humps and long necks these seemed to be strangely clumsy beasts to those unaccustomed to them, but the natives knew well how to use them and with their large feet and ability go for long periods without water, they were ideally suited to the shifting sands of the desert. As Hassan soon taught me they were of two kinds, the one like our draught oxen, slow and able to carry heavy loads for long distances and those of a lighter leaner variety, fast and able to cover the desert at an amazing speed.

Our own horses, versed in the skills of fighting with a knight in full armour, were heavily handicapped in the desert sands. The myriad flies tormented them, and the forage we obtained for them frequently seemed to disagree with them, for the grasses were very different from those they were accustomed to at home. It was necessary also to provide them with tents as shelter from the hot sun and flies. Even so many of them sickened and died including my own bay stallion Beau, despite all my efforts to save him. All in all we soon saw that we would have to adapt our ways of fighting to suit these surroundings.

"When you get down to it we seldom fight a real battle," explained one Frankish squire who had witnessed the siege of Tyre. "The Saracens are no match for a knight in armour. On the other hand wearing full armour in these conditions makes it difficult to fight properly. Chain mail is the heaviest it is really sensible to wear in this heat. The result is that it is mostly a question of besieging a fortress and eventually starving them into submission. Of course the Saracens play some rude heathen tricks. They use Greek Fire to repel attacks. Also they frequently make a point of crucifying their prisoners in full view of our lines."

"What exactly is their Greek Fire made of?" asked Alan. "I am told they use more than ordinary pitch."

"There are parts of the desert where they have pools of this oil that burns with a blue flame when lit," explained the other. "They use that or they use pitch and oil or fat extracted from animals and mix it with sulphur and other materials to make it stick to the skin, then set light to it and pour it over the besiegers from the castle walls. It is not a nice sight to see a man in armour on fire, or to hear him scream."

We both shuddered mildly at the thought. Even being burned by the midday sun baking down on uncovered chain mail or armour was bad enough, as we had all discovered already. The thought of actual flames enveloping a suit of armour with a man inside was almost too horrible to contemplate. The Frankish squire was pleased with the effect of his words.

"They also hurl burning bucketfuls of Greek fire from the walls with vast machines," he added with relish. "They can throw them several hundred yards and then without any warning you can suddenly find yourself on fire in a sea of sticky flames." (*It appears that phosphorus bombs and flamethrowers so often depicted as the product of modern 'civilised warfare' are really rather old hat. When you get down to basics, warfare is not something that can be conducted by 'civilised' rules, as the wars in Europe, the Far East, Vietnam and the*

Balkans, amongst others, have demonstrated in this century. Come to that from Gleneil's comments the Code of Chivalry did not work very well in his day either.)

It sounded to both of us as if besieging a Saracen stronghold was a far cry from the chivalrous warfare we had prepared for in Scotland. However my old mentor at Beaulieu's words came back to me. Dougal always ended up in the same way: "Now just you remember this! All this talk of chivalry is all very well in its place in the jousting ring or the tourney, but when you get down to it real battle is a brutal business and it's you against the other man, and if you don't win then you're dead! So you just remember all the little tricks I tell you and make sure you win." (*This advice from an old sweat who had been through the ranks might have come from a Roman Centurion in front of Hadrian's Wall or from a Sergeant major in the SAS in the Gulf War or any professional NCO in any other war in between.*)

Despite the news that Saladin's forces had withdrawn to Acre and that our army was besieging him, there seemed little urgency in our preparations. For the first month or so we found time enough for exploring the countryside and even some hunting. The desert oryx, or antelopes, were fast moving quarry, but, with locally bred gazehounds and mounted on the small but swift Saracen horses, good sport could be enjoyed. The King, my father, when he arrived, was soon introduced to the sport, and with my Lord Dewrie we enjoyed many good hunts in the early morning or evening, when the heat of the day was not too great.

It was sometimes difficult to make out the standing of the Eastern Frankish knights, which could easily enough lead to misunder-standings. Alan and I were taking a glass of wine out of the heat of the sun in a tent in the market, when a tall Eastern Frankish man of light colouring dressed in a dark silken gown joined us.

"Are you with King William of Scotland," he asked us.

"We are," replied Alan in his usual direct manner. "And who are you with?"

"Since Guy de Lusignan led the Eastern Frankish knights against Saladin and was proclaimed King of Jerusalem I have been by his side," he claimed rather grandly. "I am a kinsman of his, but I can also claim descent from the great hero of Roncévalles, Roland himself. My name is Éttiénne, but I am generally known to my friends as Tiénné."

"Where do you hail from?" continued Alan.

"I have certain commercial interests stretching from as far as Solomon's famed mines in deepest Africa to bazaars in Syria," replied the other loftily. "I have recently come from Jerusalem, where Guy de Lusignan had promised me the bazaar known as Herod's, but I have only recently learned to my disgust that the brothers Phayeed have acquired control of it by bribing many of the officials concerned then forging Guy de Lusignan's authority and presenting it to Saladin himself, who honoured it unaware of the deception involved. Such men are not fit to run a stall, let alone a bazaar of such widespread repute which makes such good financial returns."

I was forcibly reminded by all this of Jamie Douglas's pointed comment one evening at court after dinner when a certain weasel-faced Lord Comyn had been glorifying his ancestry and bemoaning the loss of one of his domains to a rival of equally dubious background:

"It's aye the alley cat or the half-bred cur which has been chased away from the fireside by its like that yowls the loudest."

"Are they any relation of the Mohammed el Phayeed who claims to be descended from all the Pharoahs and controls the bazaar here in Tyre?" asked Alan.

"That's the chief rogue himself" replied the Frankish knight angrily. "His brother Mahomed controls the bazaar in Acre. Between them they have a considerable commercial Empire supporting both Saladin and the Crusaders, all built on fraud. They are neither of them to be trusted and they thrive on the war, making a profit from both sides."

"I think we may have met the man," I said, interested to hear more of this. "A fat always smiling fellow, who lives close to his bazaar in Tyre?"

"That's him, all right," replied the other eagerly. "And his brother's the dead spit of him. Mo and Ma Phayeed. A more unscupulous pair you'll never meet, There isn't anything those two will not do. They supply the armies of both Saladin and the Crusaders. Whoever wins in the end they will make a fortune. It makes me fume to think of it. They live by fraud and bribery and they don't mind who they deal with, even the devil himself, I daresay. They'd probably offer St Peter a brown canvas walletful of gold to open the gates of Heaven for them."

(*There is something faintly familiar in all this. The artful skulduggery of conniving merchants or entrepreneurs and their methods of doing business seems to have changed little over the centuries.*)

"You sound rather envious," said Alan, who had perhaps drunk rather more wine in the heat of the day than was wise. "And from what you say, you seem to be in much the same line of business yourself."

"I'll not have my name coupled in any way with the brothers Phayeed," snorted the Frank, drawing his scimitar.

Fortunately the tent where we were drinking was well carpeted and the one on which he was standing ended at my feet. Seeing my friend about to be threatened in this way, I simply bent and tugged the end of the carpet with all my strength. Although a large man, his feet shot from under him and he ended an ignominious heap on the floor. His scimitar flew out of his hand and I put my foot firmly on it.

"You are speaking to the man who threw a walletful of gold at Mohammed Phayeed when he tried to offer it to him," I said forcefully. "In view of what you say I would have thought you would rather drink with him than draw a sword on him."

Éttiénne Roland seemed somewhat disconcerted by my words and as he picked himself up the murderous glare he had turned on Alan was now transferred to me. Then it seemed the meaning of my words dawned on him. He turned back to Alan and embraced him.

"Anyone who has ever thrown anything at that rogue Phayeed is a friend of mine for ever," he said fervently. "I, Tiénné Roland, have spoken."

He then turned and picked up his scimitar. With a final baleful look at me he thrust it into his waistband and then with a bow to Alan left the tent.

"I don't think you're his closest friend," Alan remarked. "But then

I don't think either he or Mohammed Phayeed, or for that matter his brother, worry much about friends. They're probably too busy counting their money and their enemies."

We ourselves soon found that it was dangerous to move around the camp at night unless in pairs and well armed. The area was full of footpads and ruffians who would attack the unwary from the shadows without warning. Alan and I were twice set upon when returning to the camp at night, but gave a good account of ourselves, in the first instance wounding two of our four would-be assailants and forcing them to run for it. On the second occasion the timely arrival of some friends enabled us to drive off a much larger band of cuthroats. Whether either of these attacks were inspired, as Hassan suggested, by Mohammed Phayeed, or were merely a part of the local scene we neither knew nor cared. With the careless confidence of youth we were sure we could look after ourselves.

Such was the scene we found on our arrival in the Holy Land. We had arrived full of zest and eager to strike a blow for Christianity against the Saracens but, after a short while we found ourselves wilting in the heat and gradually slipping into the careless idle attitude of mind which seemed to afflict anyone from the West. In a matter of a month or so we were burned as brown by the sun as any Moor, and wearing to the manner born the loose flowing garments of the East, which on our arrival we had so derided, while eyeing new arrivals from the West with the same amusement that we had encountered ourselves on our arrival.

(*A somewhat similar metamorphosis arose in the Middle East during the last war when the British Army adopted highly unmilitary garb. The officers tended to wear silk scarves, corduroy trousers and suede desert boots, also known as brothel creepers. Considerable deviations from the orthodox uniform worn were also common in the Peninsular War, although then it was largely due to military stores being in short supply and the army having to make do with whatever was available. On the other hand the same thing was common enough in India from the earliest days when the army was under the control of the East India Company. Perhaps these were just early manifestations of the independence of authority the British soldier tends to feel when abroad, beyond the*

hammed el Phayeed denied all knowledge of anything to do with the attack or its planning.

"There must be some mistake. It is a conspiracy against me," he explained with an expressive shrug of his shoulders and his usual ingratiating smile. "It is no doubt my twin brother Mahomed, who runs the bazaar in Acre, who must have been responsible for this. He has an admiration of the Saracens which I have never shared. All we have in common is our shares of the bazaar Herod's in Jerusalem. Nor, it must be said, do either of us admit there is any truth in the evil allegations put about by that Frankish imposter Roland that we did not pay the full price that was agreed, or that we did not have the money in the first place. It is a conspiracy on his part. So is this suggestion that I was any part of any Saracen plot. I personally would never put any Norman, Frankish or English knights at risk in any way. My admiration for them is complete. Also for the Scots too, of course."

There was little anyone could say in the circumstances. It was always possible that I had confused the names Mohammed and Mahomed, which to our ears sounded similar enough. Furthermore the man was undoubtedly a prominent local citizen and appeared to keep the bazaar under good control. There was little doubt that he was a rogue and a trickster, but I could not help recalling Jamie Douglas's comment:

"Once a horse thief has stolen enough horses, he may start breeding them. He may then become a highly respected horse breeder, but he can still be hung as a thief. It all depends who is judging him. Those he has stolen horses from may want to hang him, but those who have bought the horses he bred may prefer to let stolen horses continue to breed."

My own absence had apparently not been discovered until the following day and had not been considered in any way worrying then, since it was thought I must have gone off with Hassan, of whom there was still no trace. No-one had reported seeing anything of him, but, trying to find a small Nubian urchin was as hopeless as looking for a grain of sand in the desert. Who had sent the message supposedly from Alan remained a mystery. Nor, though I did my best to remember, could I recall whose voice it was I had heard before I was hit on the head. My mind remained obstinately blank.

It was not until I had been recognised as I was about to be nailed to the cross that anyone had even realised that I had been captured. My subsequent escape with the bloody sword held at the Caliph's throat was a nine day wonder, and my knighthood was generally felt to be well earned. I was glad enough, however, when, a week or so later, a determined sally by the Saracens resulted in a pitched battle for once, and we all had something else to occupy our minds.

Meanwhile my life had become irrevocably changed. My Lord Dewrie, whose appearance had so shocked me on my return developed the shaking sickness, and after a week of the tremors and sweating, despite copious bleeding and cupping, died. The young Caliph Haroun el Fahid proved to be an extremely wealthy man in a land where riches were commonplace. He decreed his own ransom as his weight in gold and jewels, but since he had not yet reached his full growth he threw in the weight of his horse as well. I confess at the time to a feeling of regret that the Saracen horses did not match our own chargers for size, but the resulting treasure, when it finally arrived, was enough to pay the King my father's debts, which were considerable and also to assure me of all I could desire from life. From being a penniless young squire and bastard son of the royal blood I was suddenly a Knight with all the wealth I could desire and a figure of some consequence in my father's court. For a start I was able to take on the men-at-arms and followers of my Lord Dewrie, and Alan, my erstwhile boon companion, became my squire.

Ours was a longstanding friendship and our new relationship made little difference to our life. He had almost always been the one to keep note of our needs and requirements. He it was who had almost always kept me informed of our engagements. Now we soon settled down to much our old ways with the slight difference that I always automatically took the blame when things went wrong. John Weir, as my Master-at-Arms, was the man who ran our small company smoothly and in him I had a devoted follower for he still considered I had saved his life when he was about to be washed overboard, although in truth he would have done as much for me as I told him at the time.

One of the more surprising things to result from my sudden change of fortune was a quickly developing friendship with my captive Caliph, the young Haroun el Fahid. He was a young man of much my own age with many tastes in common and once he had given his word not to try to escape, while awaiting the arrival of his ransom, he was treated at my father's court more as an honoured guest than a prisoner. I had admired his stance at my trial when he had argued the case for leniency. He in turn confessed freely that he had admired my feat in starting the avalanche which trapped the Nubian guards. He bore me no grudge for capturing him as I had and showed a remarkable composure throughout, which even those who loathed all Saracens had to admire.

With Alan and myself, the three of us, all much of an age, hunted the oryx and flew our falcons at the sand grouse and bustards. Mounted on his splendid stallion Haroun el Fahid was a hard man to follow, but when it came to testing each other at arms we found our ways completely different. He wore only the lightest chain mail and was armed merely with a round metal shield and a scimitar. This was a beautifully balanced weapon, easy to handle, but useless against a suit of armour.

Alan was particularly scornful of the latter weapon when he first handled it, but he had not seen at close quarters two heads severed cleanly from their necks with two successive strokes with hardly any effort involved. Even so he should have appreciated more clearly the perfect balance and the sharpness of the cutting edge of the Caliph's weapon, which had a heavily inlaid gold and silver handle encrusted with emeralds and rubies.

"Watch how our two handed swords cut through iron," Alan said, laying an iron bar between two pieces of wood, then swinging his sword down with a powerful overhand stroke and severing the bar neatly in half. "Can your sword do that?"

"Perhaps not," replied Haroun el Fahid, with a cool smile. "But can your sword do this?"

He threw up a silken cushion on which he was resting and cut it neatly in half with one swift blow, sending feathers flying in a shower through the air. It was an interesting demonstration of the difference in our styles of warfare. The Saracens depended on speed and lightness, whereas the Crusaders, for the most part, were slow and ponderous in their armour, but an almost irresistible force. It was a contrast in differing ways of fighting and explanation enough in itself why it was largely a war of sieges rather than battles. It also explained why when we did meet in battle, especially with our superiority in bowmen, we usually were triumphant. It was principally against Eastern Knights armed much like themselves that Saladin's forces had triumphed. The only reason the Crusaders did not sweep all before them was simply the difficulty of moving an army through the deserts and inhospitable rocky regions which seemed to make up so much of the Holy Land. The Saracens had the big advantage of being able to move swiftly through the deserts regions and knowing how to live off the land.

(*It was the desert and the landscape which largely dictated the strategy in the 1939–45 War. Even a modern army with all the advantages of air and naval support found it extremely difficult to move in the desert. Neither side was helped by the fact that those back in Europe and Britain were apparently unable to understand the conditions under which their armies were fighting. Once either army had gained a major victory and advanced several hundred miles the difficulties of keeping them supplied multiplied accordingly. The wear and tear on men and machinery in the desert conditions was very considerable and keeping both in good condition and well supplied with food and ammunition was the major problem. The Crusaders faced much the same difficulties, but instead of two European forces facing each other they were up against the Saracens who knew the ways of the desert intimately. Despite their seeming advantage in battle the Crusaders were bound to have found it a hard struggle just to survive. Quite apart from those who died in battle there must have been many who contracted diseases such as malaria, dysentery, cholera and leprosy to name only a few. It is really remarkable not just that any returned home to Britain, but that any survived at all. They must have been remarkably tough.*)

While Haroun el Fahid was still with us another tourney was

held, as much to relieve the boredom of the siege as anything else. With the loss of so many of their best troops the garrison of Acre it was clear were unlikely to spring any fresh surprises and indeed, despite Saladin's orders to the contrary, there had already been negotiations for surrender. So it was that the prospect of another tourney raised everyone's spirits considerably.

Every attraction that could possibly be provided in these circumstances was organised. There were booths and sideshows, jugglers and mountebanks. There were tents offering every delight that the East could provide, from snake charmers to belly dancers. There were stalls providing kebabs, roasted kid and lamb, and wonderfully spiced delicacies. Yet other stalls offered every type of silk or leather garments. There were archery contests and bowls and skittles for the less gifted. It was a feast for the eyes and for the purse, but I could not help feeling very unlike the tourney at Beaulieu. Alan and I laughed together at the thought of Donald's comments had he been present.

It was noticeable that Mohammed el Phayeed was not prepared to miss the chance of making a profit on the day. Through his many contacts amongst the Franks and Normans his stalls were offering the very best and most Frankish of clothing straight from Calais and Paris. He had been extremely incensed when Tiénné Roland had offered the Charlemagne Cup for the last Knight on his feet and the Roncévalles cup for the finest horn blower on the day and so he himself had offered a special gold 'Herod's Cup' for the 'most parfait gentil Knight.' The rules, on how this cup was to be won were complex and unclear and the donor seemed not to care particularly about the details of how it was won. He was content he announced for it to be presented by King Richard himself. It was noticeable, however, that he always made a point of being seen as prominently as possible in the background whenever King Richard happened to be near the Cup.

(*This sounds like an unholy combination between an Agricultural Show, a Game Fair, a Football match and a Show Jumping event with a touch of Derby Day thrown in. It was obviously an explosive mixture, if ever there was one. Unfortunately Gleneil does not record who won the prizes he mentions, but in view of his previous comments it seems more than possible that Guy de Lusignan was the recipient of the gold cup.*)

Despite my dislike of suits of armour and preference for chain mail, I had had, perforce, to have the smiths measure me and make me a suit. The first time I wore it in actual combat was in this tourney, when I took my part with half a dozen Scots knights, of whom James Macdonnel armed with his favourite weapon the morning-star was one, against an equal number of English knights. It started with each pair of Knights making a mounted tilt in the lists in which I was fortunate to unhorse my opponent. In the ensuing melee, however, I had barely had time to exchange more than a few effective sword strokes before I received a sudden unexpected blow on the side of my helm which unhorsed me and laid me low. As I lay for a few seconds dazed I heard a familiar voice cry in triumph.

"Got the little bastard!"

The effect of the blow combined with the words was strange in the extreme. For a moment it was as if I was back there still climbing the rope and looking down at the clouds of dust rising from the floor of the Wadi Halifa just after starting the avalanche. It was as if time stood still for a moment as memory flooded back and I knew it was James Macdonnel's voice that had been so familiar. The memory was so strong that for a moment I could not think where I was, or how I came to be on my knees in a suit of armour in the middle of a melee which now appeared to be nearing its end, for as my vision cleared I saw there were only three left standing.

Already the English supporters on the sidelines were howling abuse and fighting with rival Scots supporters. In addition there were Norman and Frankish spectators and numerous others joining in the general melee. Those who had laid wagers and lost were complaining of cheating and those who had laid wagers and won were demanding their gold. In places the fighting had already almost extended into the tourney ground itself, although the squires and men-at-arms and other stewards were still successful in holding them back from invading the ground itself. (*This is a remarkably familiar scenario, very similar to the scenes at professional bare-fisted fights in the 19th century and at football matches today. No doubt the Roman mobs watching gladiators in the Colosseum behaved in much the same way. Human nature and human emotions in certain circumstances, like the human innards, cf the Tripoli Trots above, do not alter greatly, however 'advanced' we may claim to be today. Mob rule led by yobboes of any age, race, colour, or for that matter sex, for this is not a sexist issue, is something that can happen wherever several hundred people are gathered together in the grip of a powerful emotion. It has happened often enough in the past and will undoubtedly happen again in the future for much the same reasons. In the grip of communal emotion raised to fever pitch common sense and control disappear entirely and a group becomes a mob. This is particularly the case in a hot climate or where alcohol or drugs have been circulating freely, loosening the inhibitions and removing the veneer of civilisation, which normally acts as a block against civil disorder. In some cases it may be deliberately orchestrated by trouble-makers, but in others it may be completely spontaneous It does not augur well for the time when football is played in tropical climates. It also perhaps explains why it is that football riots are uncommon in Iceland or Scandinavia.)*

I struggled to my feet and saw James standing a few paces away. He was engaged with two English knights who were pressing him hard, but he was holding them at bay with his favourite weapon, the weighty spiked ball of the morning-star on its chain. I learned later that it was this that had unhorsed me in the melee, although it had been skilfully done. Alan told me subsequently that to all outward appearances it was a back-hand blow from behind, which had merely landed on the wrong target, something that was all too easy in those circumstances.

I stepped forward and took my place beside him and swung my sword in an overarm stroke which took the nearest English knight on the helm and weak though the blow undoubtedly was it went home and proved enough to fell him. James with a successful final swing of his favourite weapon at the same moment laid low the other and we stood facing each other both of us swaying with the effort of our exertions and both of us, I daresay, somewhat shaken. Certainly I know my legs felt very weak and barely able to support me. I was leaning on my sword and breathing heavily. James was facing me in very much the same sorry state.

The cheers and jeers of the spectators had now reached fever pitch and I was dimly aware of fighting going on all round the tourney ground. The stewards were doing their best to hold back the varlets and camp followers and assorted spectators who were struggling on the fringes of the ground, but were slowly giving way. It was obvious it could not be long before the ground was invaded by the mass of struggling humanity

I pushed up the visor of my helm and James did likewise and we stared at each other for a long moment. I felt somehow as if I was seeing him for the first time and that this was a stranger who stood before me, whom I had never met before. He, in his turn, must have seen from my expression that I knew, for he went first white and then red as he stared back at me, his face twisting into an expression of hate and fury.

"It was you!" I said accusingly.

He answered me with a mixture of vindictiveness and triumph in his voice and his face contorted into an unattractive sneer.

"You were on the end of a rope once too often, weren't you" he said, spewing out the words in a rush. "And it gave me great pleasure to catch you in the act. I thought leaving you for the Saracens to deal with would be a more deserving end than simply cutting the rope and letting you swing into space, but it seems you have more lives than a cat."

"What did you do with Hassan?" I demanded

"You mean the Saracen brat, I suppose," he replied. "I left him with the camel herder too. I don't know what happened to him, but I hoped they would make sure of you at least. I will just have to do the task myself, I suppose."

As he said the last words I saw his body turning as he swung and I realised he was aiming a blow at my helm. I raised my arm and broke the strength of the blow at the same time butting my head forward onto his chest. The force of the blows unbalanced us both and we fell in a tangle of arms and legs on the ground. We each received a faceful of sand through our open helms and sat up spluttering and spitting.

By this time Alan and the other squires were on the ground assisting their masters, while the fighting supporters of the various sides had now invaded the tourney ground. I had no further chance of conversation with James, nor did I wish for it. Truth to tell I was still more than a little dazed and as Alan helped me from the ground I realised that blood was trickling down my shoulder from the blow on my head. I soon realised I also had a considerable number of bruises in various parts of my body. As Alan gently helped me to remove the armour I saw the helm had a large dent towards the back. The damage, however, was little more than skin missing from a patch of my forehead where my head had jarred against the visor.

"It was James Macdonnel at the Wadi Halifa," I told Alan as he helped me onto a palliasse where he proceeded to rub unguents and salves into the more obvious bruises I had received.

"Oh! So that was what you were talking about at the end of the tourney before he tried to brain you with his morning star and you both fell down," said Alan. "I thought it might be something like that. You looked as if you were squaring up to each other like a pair of fighting cocks. I doubt if many people watching in the pavilions or on the sidelines realised it, but I was close enough to see it was no accident. The man must be mad!"

"Obsessed, certainly," I agreed, acknowledging the truth at last.

"That bell rope has a lot to answer for," remarked Alan with a grim smile. "It's brought you near to death more than once."

"I think it goes back further than that," I replied. "The death of the Boar was the start of it. That was when it all began."

"It could have been, I suppose," admitted Alan. "In which case he's had all the longer to brood on it."

"It must have been him that sent the message supposedly from you," I went on. "I should never have been fooled so easily. It was stupid of me."

"I think you blame yourself too much," replied Alan. "It was reasonable enough to receive a message from me. He was just very lucky that he arrived at the right moment."

"Or else he was lying in wait," I said thoughtfully. "Suppose he had been told that an attack was intended, and knew that the Wadi would be full of Nubian troops? Then he knew I was bound to hear them and would go over to look down at them. He more or less said he had originally intended just to push me over the edge."

"Who would have been able to tell him something like that in advance?" enquired Alan thoughtfully. "Someone who has a foot in both camps perhaps?."

"Mohammed el Phayeed!" we both said together.

"He's always accusing others of conspiracies against him," went on Alan triumphantly. "So who more likely to be a conspirator himself?"

"That's true enough, but whoever it was scarcely matters. If it was Mohammed, and I grant you that seems most likely, he's certainly not going to admit it." I said, recovering first. "The point is what do I do about James? If I accuse him of it outright he only has to deny it all and what proof have I got beyond the fact that he has admitted it to me? I daresay he would have a dozen of his followers claim on oath that he could not have done it."

"The King, your father, would take your word against his if you were to put it before him," protested Alan.

"I do not intend to bring my father into this," I answered, obstinately. "This is between James and myself. As I see it I have no option. I will have to challenge him to meet me in mortal combat. This is something that must be settled for once and for all."

Alan, who had been oiling my ribs, looked at me for a moment, and then rolled me over onto my face so that he could attend to my back.

"In that case I suppose you will be expecting me to throw down the gauntlet for you?" he demanded, applying a dollop of unguent to my back and massaging it home with unnecessary vigour. "Just don't forget that he can be a good fighter, as you saw today, and he's up to every trick that's known and won't mind using any foul means to win if he has to."

"We've both known him long enough to know that," I replied drily. "And there's no need to add any more bruises to my back than are there already."

So it was that the following night, while we feasted in the King my father's tent after the tourney, Alan entered holding my metal gauntlet in his hand. He marched down to James Macdonnel's seat at the table and cast it down with a clatter amongst the dishes before him.

"My lord, Sir Iain Gleneil of Gleneil challenges you to mortal combat," he announced loudly.

There was a sudden hush in the general hubbub of conversation as those up and down the table craned their heads to see what was happening. James Macdonnel put down the cup from which he was drinking and stared at Alan with his old familiar supercilious gaze. Then he looked up across the room and saw me looking at him from a seat near my father. His face underwent the same ugly transformation I had seen earlier on the tourney field. His colour changed from white to choleric red, and his mouth twisted in that same unbecoming sneer.

"It is a pity that so promising a knight should die so young," he replied, with a curl of his lip. "But presumptuous puppies must be taught their lessons. I will send my squire to agree the time and place."

I was reminded of an old saying of Jamie Douglas;

"A cock may crow on top of the dung heap as long as it pleases and be as contemptuous of the young cocks as it may, but once it has to come down and fight it's a different matter. Experience is aye useful but youth, strength, guts and sheer determination will win the day every time. The old cock may think it's learned the tricks of fighting, but if the young cock goes at him regardless and is strong and determined enough that's that."

For a long moment James stared across the tables at me then his eyes dropped. I was conscious of the hate that emanated from him and, surprisingly, instead of reciprocating it. I found myself aware once again of that feeling of loss I had experienced years before when he had marched away from me after the death of the Great Boar. Then gradually the conversation picked up again and soon the feasting and revelries were in full swing once more.

I left the banquet early, and returned to my tent where Alan was waiting for me.

"It is all arranged," he said. "The day after tomorrow. As the challenged he has the choice of weapons, and he has chosen the morning-star and swords. Full armour and dismounted."

That was more or less what I had expected. Being dismounted meant that he had the advantage of weight and size. The choice of morning-star, known to be his favourite weapon with which he was very experienced, and broad sword was probably more in his favour than mine. On the other hand apart from choosing a mounted start I could not complain. All said and done, when it comes to killing or being killed one weapon is much like another.

I found surprisingly that once the decision was made my spirits lifted. I took Alan and Haroun el Fahid for a morning ride in the desert when we found an outlying oryx and had an exhilarating hunt behind the hounds with the oryx itself, a fine young buck with a grand pair of horns, eventually escaping along the face of a wadi. It was a fine morning and we were three young men, much of an age, and all of us enjoying the freshness of the morning air and the pure exhilaration of keeping up at full gallop while watching two animals pitting their strengths and wits against each other at speed in the wild

"Ha, my friend," cried Haroun el Fahid, as we halted our sweating horses and watched the buck disappear triumphantly in a series of bounds across the wadi face. "It is good to be alive is it not?"

I caught the glance which passed between Alan and him as he realised the inappropriateness of the remark in front of one destined to mortal combat the following day. Such was my own feeling of enjoyment in the chase at that moment that I laughed aloud from sheer exuberance.

"Don't pull long faces on my behalf, Alan," I cried. "Haroun el Fahid is right. It was a great chase, and the buck remains to be hunted another day. I trust that right will triumph tomorrow, and that I too will live to hunt another day, but there is no point in dwelling on it. Let us enjoy ourselves while we may."

In truth it was soon too hot to hunt any longer and we returned to the camp. There Alan insisted that I should have a rest and further massage for the bruising I had taken in the tourney. I told him that he was fussing like an old hen with its chick, but I have to admit I felt better for his ministrations. Then, as usual, we rested during the heat of the day, and finally after a light evening meal I retired early to bed. I cannot say that I slept particularly well, but at least I slept, and when Alan wakened me at dawn I felt fresh enough and ready for the worst that James could offer.

After a light meal of a good bloody beef steak and a braised chicken followed by a cool drink of lemon, for there was no ale to be had in the Holy Land and I did not feel like drinking wine, I had a short mock swordplay with Alan to ease my arms and legs. Then I donned my chain mail with only a helm as protection from the blows of the morning star. I had discussed this with Alan and he agreed with me that speed and freedom of movement was better in single combat rather than the overall protection of a full suit of armour, which necessarily slowed the wearer's actions. This was sometimes seen in mock combat, but not otherwise. On the other hand there were no strict rules on the matter and I felt the advantage would be with me. Whether it was this thought or the sight of Alan's long face as we rode from our tent to the tourney ground I do not know, but I felt quite lighthearted and not at all like a man about to fight for his life.

In the shadow on the other side of the ground James's small party were already present when we arrived, although we ourselves were in ample time. He was already dressed in full armour and although his back was turned to me I could see his distinctive red hair as he bent his head and his squire helped him on with his helm. I made haste to our stance at the other end of the ground, and there Alan helped me on with my helm.

"Just don't let him get to close quarters," repeated Alan anxiously, yet again.

"I know," I repeated impatiently. "I have the advantage of lightness. That's why I chose chain mail instead of armour."

We were probably both getting a little edgy, and it was a relief when James's squire came over to confer with Alan.

"We've agreed that three blasts on a horn will signify the start," reported Alan. "After that it is to the death."

There was a somewhat final ring to these words, but I suppose I was too on edge to notice it. Up to that moment I had been feeling tremors in my knees and legs, and had been hoping that Alan had not noticed and put the wrong construction on them. Now that there was the immediate prospect of action they miraculously vanished and I felt ready, even eager, for the fight.

With a pat on the back from Alan and a muttered 'Good luck' I walked forward towards the centre of the tourney field. I could see James advancing from the opposite side and as we approached each other the horn blew three times. When we were within a few paces of each other and still out of range of each other we both stopped and circled each other cautiously, each looking for an opening.

James kept his morning-star well forward swinging it in a circular motion clockwise below his waist. I took the correct counter swinging mine counter-clockwise and by my side. As we edged round each other James, constricted by his armour, was much slower, and I found as I had expected that I could move and feint with much greater ease. I managed thus to get in two good blows to his left arm, for I was using the accepted tactics of concentrating on one spot, preferably an arm joint to curtail his movements, but then he managed a quick return, which caught me almost full on the shoulder. It was a well aimed blow and, even though I managed to twist sideways to evade the full force of it, I staggered several paces before recovering my balance. I knew that I could not afford to take many more like it. I could feel my left arm grow numb, and was aware I would not be able to use it as freely as before. I was determined, however, not to let him realise the effect of the blow, and continued to circle him without showing any sign of pain.

With the lighter chain mail I was able to move faster on my feet, which as I had hoped was a considerable advantage. We were both fighting with our visors up as was the custom for there was little danger of a blow from the morning-star hitting the helm and damaging our faces, and the advantage of a better range of vision this provided more than made up for that unlikely possibility. It was however because of this that I nearly fell victim to a well known if underhand trick which James played on me.

I had caught him another light blow on the side and had just stepped backwards a pace or two when he appeared to stagger and put one hand to the ground. I naturally moved forward to take advantage of a possible opening when he thrust his arm forward and threw a handful of sand into my face. Fortunately my head was slightly turned so that I was only temporarily blinded in one eye and I was able to repel the attack that followed with only one heavy blow to the shoulder and another to the ribs. After that I was able to slip back out of range of further punishment, though still with the vision in the one eye somewhat impaired.

It was not long. however, before I had completely recovered and the trick in turn gave me an idea. I continued for the next four or five attacks to concentrate on striving for a blow at his visor. Eventually I managed to land a heavy blow exactly on the joint of the visor itself. I was pleased to see that as a result it had slipped down and his efforts to thrust it back into place were no use. As I had hoped the consequence was that he was now being forced to fight not only with full armour, but with the difficulty of impaired vision, having to peer through the slits in his visor.

During the combat itself I was unaware of the passage of time, but I am told we continued thus, without any further decisive blows being struck, for getting on for the best part of an hour. The sun by now was up and of course we each tried to manoeuvre the other so that the sun was in his eyes before we put in an attack. It was also growing hotter by the moment, and I could feel the sweat soaking through my tunic. Chain mail was bad enough, but I knew that in his armour James would be suffering even more.

Eventually the moment came that I had been waiting for; James I noticed had been getting careless in his guard. His morning-star was revolving slowly on its chain and, suddenly increasing the revolutions of mine, I slipped forward a pace and catching his chain with mine behind the morning-star successfully locked our chains together. With a quick step backwards and a heave I jerked the weapon free from his grasp and had him disarmed. I swung the awkward weapon round and attempted a blow at his head before he could draw his sword. Although I caught him on the helm and knocked him backwards it was not a heavy blow. He staggered backward a couple of paces and started to draw his sword.

I had the choice of trying for another blow or drawing my sword also. Rightly or wrongly I threw the clumsier weapon aside and drew my sword also. Alan told me later that he groaned aloud as he saw me throw away what seemed to him my advantage. However I knew that my shoulder was too numb by now to do well with the morning-star whereas I have always felt more at ease with the sword.

Apart from feeling happier with the sword, with the greater mobility provided by my chain mail I was sure I now had a distinct advantage. It was only when I came to swing experimentally towards the left hand that I appreciated that the blow to my shoulder had left me distinctly weak on that side. On the other hand I saw that the greater weight of his armour and the length of time we had been fighting were beginning to tell on James. Aware that he had hit me hard on the left shoulder, however, he pressed me on that side. For a while he attacked steadily, swinging his sword two handed at my left side, and I was hard put to defend myself. I also now had to lower my own visor so that it seemed all the advantage I had gained before was now lost.

The effort we had both expended during this spell had left me dripping with sweat and half blinded at times inside my helm as I peered through my visor. James, I felt sure, could be in no better state, since I had managed several shrewd blows to his head, and I could see him staggering once or twice as he moved to attack. It was in one of these attacks that I managed to evade his blow completely and he swung past me exposing his head and body unguarded. I swung round a two handed blow with all my force behind it and caught him full on the join of his visor. I felt the blow right down my arms and a stab of pain lanced through my shoulder. I knew I must have pulled a muscle or broken something, but I was also aware with a momentary feeling of savage triumph that my sword had gone home through his helm.

I saw him stagger backwards and felt my sword pulled with him as a gout of blood spewed forth from his helm over my blade. He dropped his sword and his knees folded as he fell backwards onto the ground. Whether I had killed him or not, I knew he would not be able to continue the fight. Even had I had the strength to do so I had no desire to carry it any further. The fleeting feeling of triumph I had experienced, as I made that final blow, had passed as quickly as it came. I felt a tremendous lassitude creeping over me, and I had considerable difficulty in disengaging my sword from his helm. It was firmly embedded in the metal and at first I could not summon up the power to move it. I had at last to put a foot on his chest and pull with all my remaining strength before it would come loose, and another gout of blood came with it welling from the damaged visor.

Although he had given a groan as the sword first struck there was no sound or movement from him now and it seemed obvious to me, from the amount of blood coming from his helm, that it had been a fatal stroke. I did not feel there was any point in carrying out the formal rites of removing his helm and demanding his surrender on pain of chopping off his head, even if I had had the strength left to do so. If he was not dead it seemed to me clear he was deeply unconscious and dying. I felt no elation at the thought that James was now dead by my hand. I felt instead once more that sense of loss I had felt so many years before. I was also suddenly conscious of feeling extremely weary, and I became aware that I was swaying on my feet so that it was a relief to have Alan's supporting hand under my arm.

I did not wait to see James's body carried from the field. Alan and Haroun el Fahid, one on each side, supported me back to my tent. There Alan attended to me, seeing to my bruises and clucking like a hen over my shoulder. This he decided was no more than a fractured collar bone, rather than the shoulder blade itself, but he bound me up and eased my other aches and pains with ointments and unguents. A draught of wine and a light meal and I began to feel myself again. It appeared that the King, my father, had watched the combat and reportedly had been duly pleased with my conduct. I was bidden to join his court that evening.

Strangely enough I did not feel any sense of triumph. Rather it was as if a void had opened in my life. I had known James so long that even the awareness of his hatred of me was something that seemed to have been there always. I had not really wished to fight him. By his own actions he had forced it on me. Now that it was over I had this strange sense of loss. He had undoubtedly been my enemy as he had proved only too well, but he seemed somehow a part of my youth. Perhaps it is ever thus when one finally enters manhood.

At dinner that evening the King, my father, made much of me and I had a great deal more wine than I would have wished. The Macdonnels who had always previously been prominent at court next to the Frasers were conspicuous now by their absence. It was clearly understood that with the death of James, the eldest son of their chief and his representative on the Crusade they would be returning home at once. While they were good fighters and some loss to the Scots force this was understandable enough in the circumstances.

Chapter 7

The Return to Gleneil

The siege of Acre did not last much longer. After negotiations, which continued for a couple of months, the Governor agreed to surrender terms against the express orders of Saladin. By the terms of surrender Acre was to remain unpillaged and the inhabitants were granted amnesty. This caused a certain amount of ill-feeling amongst the Crusaders' camp, since looting and pillage were considered only reasonable perquisites at the successful conclusion of a siege, but it was reluctantly accepted.

Alan and I were away at the end of the siege accompanying Haroun el Fahid to his home and being feasted and fêted there in princely style. The boundaries of the land he ruled covered one of the principal trade routes to the East and, since he levied a heavy tax on every caravan of merchants passing through, he was surpassingly wealthy. It was an interesting experience and a full three months before he would allow us to return laden not only with the ransom he had promised but numerous presents as well.

On our return I personally found it an interesting experience to re-trace my previous visit to Acre. I had the pleasure of repaying the kindness of the greyhaired gaoler with a gold piece and laying the flat of my sword across the backside of the scarred holder of the keys to teach him to have more thought for his prisoners.

While walking through the streets with Alan I was suddenly accosted by a small figure who grasped my hand frantically.

"My lord, my lord," he cried. "Take me back! Take me back!

It was none other than the lad, Hassan, who had disappeared at the time of my abduction after the avalanche. His story was a simple one. He had been looking down, preparatory to helping me back over the cliff, when, like me, he was hit on the head. The earth-shaking sounds of the avalanche I had created had covered the sound of anyone approaching, and he had no idea of what had happened. He had been taken as a slave by the camel herder and sold at auction in Acre. There he had been bought by a merchant who had treated him well enough, but he was eager to return to my service. The merchant was willing enough to part with him for a trifling sum and he returned to the camp with us.

(Surprisingly Gleneil makes no mention of the massacre of some 2,000 Saracen prisoners which took place on Richard's direct orders after the siege of Acre. The likelihood is that he was not present at the time, since he recorded spending three months away with the young Caliph Haroun al Fahid, but this particular example of Richard's standards of chivalry compares very poorly with those of Saladin after his capture of Jerusalem when he spared all the prisoners taken. It is fairly clear that Richard must have been a natural strategist and good leader in battle since many of the Normans, Franks and others who accepted his leadership in the Crusade had little reason to like him. On the contrary he had given most of the rulers in Europe good cause either to fear and loathe him or, in the case of the Emperor Henry IV, whose authority he had persistently flouted. every reason to look for any opportunity to subdue him. Richard seems to have been a man who readily made enemies and who regarded the knightly code of chivalry as only binding on him when it suited him. He seems to have been well named Richard Yea and Nay since he obviously seldom committed himself to any direct statement and always tried to leave himself an escape clause in any agreement he made. No doubt he felt the divine right of kings gave him a right to ignore any agreement he might have made whenever he felt like it. On the other hand to be fair to him most of the other Kings and Princes in Europe at the time seem to have behaved in much the same way honouring agreements only when it suited them or when they were forced to do so. In this respect Richard does not appear to have been very much worse than many others. On the credit side, as Gleneil noted and everyone appears agreed, he seems to have been an inspiring leader in battle and a sound stategist, but his uncontrollable temper was clearly his greatest weakness. His behaviour to Duke Leopold of Austria, whom he insulted publicly and unforgiveably after the siege of

Acre, was such that he left immediately vowing to have his revenge,
which he was not long in exacting; see below).

After ending the siege of Acre, King Richard then made use of
our superior sea power and went on with a great part of the army to
secure a victory over Saladin at Jaffa, down the coast. This was
followed another successful attack on the Saracen army as they re-
grouped further south at Arsuf. Thereafter our aim was to capture
Jerusalem, but although near success on several occasions our efforts
to penetrate inland without support from the sea were not so
successful.

We Scots took our fair share of these campaigns, and the Gleneil
contingent were always in the forefront of battle. This may sound
boastful, but Alan and I learned a lot from our steady Master-at-
Arms, John Weir. To be in the forefront of the fighting has the great
advantage that you can adapt your own tactics to the situation as
required, without being ordered about by some half-fledged young
commander with no battle sense. You almost certainly do not have
the grave disadvantage of Kings or vainglorious hotheads with
banners held aloft beside you attracting all the glory seekers on
the other side, or at anyrate you can usually keep well clear of them if
they are around. If you are in the forefront you can choose a likely
weak spot to attack, and the ground is not usually strewn with
corpses of men or horses making your own approach more difficult.
Then again if you are in the forefront of the attack the enemy are
usually shooting over your head at the people behind you. If your
forces hold firm in the forefront the enemy will usually tend to move
aside and look for easier targets, and then there is every chance you
may be able to break through. If you succeed in breaking the front
ranks you then have every opportunity of exploiting the enemy's
weakness and attacking them from the side or from the rear, when
they are at a considerable disadvantage. They are then much more
likely to turn and run. The advantages of being in the forefront of
battle are in fact considerable. In the course of the campaign the
Gleneils became a fighting unit of which we were all proud. (*It is only
on going over old battlegrounds today that one realises how small an area
was usually taken up for a battle before the invention and widespread use*

of gunpowder and artillery. They were usually fought in an area not much larger than a football pitch. A small determined force fighting as a single disciplined unit in such circumstances could make a big difference in the sort of free-for-all and loose maul into which many of these battles must have degenerated. It certainly seems the Gleneils made a considerable name for themselves in just this way.)

Just as we were beginning to get into our stride, and looking forward to victory, the end came abruptly. A Treaty was negotiated with Saladin whereby access would be provided to Jerusalem and Guy de Lusignan was affirmed as King of Jerusalem. With this rather half-hearted agreement the Crusade was judged to be successfully concluded.

(Richard had been sent news of his brother John's intrigues against him back in England and had been warned that he should return home if he wished to retain his crown. This was the real reason the Crusade ended with this hastily cobbled together and rather unsatisfactory peace settlement. After little more than a year in the Holy Land Richard left Palestine in October 1192, but he was faced a major problem. Although the detention of a Crusader was contrary to public law he knew this would not deter his enemies and his position was similar to that of a mouse with two holes, each guarded by different cats. The natural route back to Toulon and thus through France was barred to him because he was well aware that the Emperor Henry IV and others he had antagonised were in wait for him there. He sailed instead up the Adriatic and tried to slip through Austria disguised as a Troubador, but the Duke Leopold was also waiting for him to exact a sweet revenge for the humiliation he had suffered at Richard's hands after the siege of Acre. His disguise penetrated, Richard was caught and imprisoned by Leopold in December 1192. Early in 1193 the Emperor Henry IV forced Leopold to pass his prisoner on to him. Richard was then only released after paying Henry homage and promising to pay a heavy ransom of 150,000 marks. In order to raise even the first instalments, which were all that was ever paid, a tax had to be introduced on movable property in England, the precursor of income tax. Richard himself was not allowed to return to England until early 1194. While he was in prison his wife Berengaria remained in Sicily and Rome, only eventually being reunited with him in 1195.)

In the company of many others I made the journey to Jerusalem, more out of curiosity I fear than any specific religious feeling. Having ventured so far I felt that it was only right to visit the place for which so many lives had been lost and so much emotion roused. Rather as I had expected I found the town full of beggars and most of the bazaars filled with little more than cheapjack souvenirs aimed at the visitors from afar. If the pieces of the true cross offered for sale were all put together they would have made a forest large enough to conceal an army.

I was interested to see the brothers Phayeed together in Jerusalem. Like two of the same mould they were almost indistinguishable from each other. Mohammed who had the bazaar in Tyre and had always claimed to be a Norman supporter, wishing nothing better than to be a Norman, looked almost exactly like his portly brother, Mahomed, who had the bazaar in Acre and claimed to be a fervent follower of Saladin. The pair of them made much of their ownership of the bazaar, Herod's, in Jerusalem, which was the cause of so much dissension with Éttiénne Roland. The rights to the bazaar it seemed had originally been promised to Éttiénne Roland by Guy de Lusignan at the start of the campaign when Richard had somewhat prematurely granted him the title of King of Jerusalem, Roland claimed that the brothers had in the meantime obtained control of the bazaar by misrepresentation and no doubt by a liberal dispensa-tion of brown canvas wallets to the various officials and others involved.

We naturally visited this much disputed bazaar, Herod's, where the brothers Mo and Ma Phayeed were very prominently in evidence, warmly greeting any visitors they considered of note. Although welcomed by both brothers as old friends, Alan and I were not very impressed by it or them, and thought the special children's bazaar nearby, called Damages, much more interesting. Athough the facts it seemed were not really in question the dispute over the ownership of the bazaar appeared destined to continue for ever, for none of the rival claimants was prepared to give way. But, since possession is always the stronger position, Tiénné Roland was forced to petition anyone who might listen to his side of the seemingly endless saga. He even sent troubadors giving his side of the story to the courts of everyone he thought might be in any position to influence the matter, but all to no avail. At the same time the brothers claimed conspiracies against them by all and sundry and Tiénné Roland in particular. Most people were driven to the cynical conclusion that they were all rogues. Then there came an unexpected outcome to the affair which left all of us except the participants themselves laughing loudly . . . (*At this point there is unfortunately a large piece of the sheepskin on which the original was written which appears to have been gnawed and eaten and since we were faced with a large gap in the manuscript, with no helpful words or phrases from which the meaning might at least have been guessed if not actually transcribed we have been forced to leave it blank. Surprisingly enough, although much more of the original has suffered damage from smaller animals such as mice, from damp, from wear and tear and from snails, moths and other insects this is the only piece clearly damaged by larger rodents, almost certainly rats. It is unfortunate that the answer to this tangled problem will never now be known but perhaps suitable that the solution to the impasse should have ended in the stomachs of predators of this kind. The words arrested, or arresting, seems to have been used several times, as do sale and plotting, but who if anyone was arrested or sold or plotted against by whom, it is no longer possible to say. After the gap we find a quotation from Jamie Douglas the court jester, which must have been apposite for it to be included but which provided no helpful answer as to what actually happened.*)

Jamie Douglas, as usual, had an appropriate comment highly relevant to the situation. "When honest men fall out in public it brings a smile to the face of the attorneys. When rogues fall out it in public it brings a smile to the face of honest men and the attorneys. Either way, mind, it's likely the attorneys will wax fat as they aye do on other people's quarrels."

Thus it was that the Third Crusade drew to a conclusion. Some may say that it was not a very satisfactory one, but then it seems to me that wars seldom do result in satisfactory conclusions, perhaps, least of all religious wars. Where there is a chance for plunder then one side at least may benefit, but when there is nothing but starvation and death then neither side gains anything. In this case I was amongst the most fortunate in the whole Crusading force, for the ransom I received from Haroun el Fahid was sufficient for me to return to Scotland and retire with my followers to Gleneil.

We took ourselves aboard a galley with all the men who had served with us. With our shared experiences we had become a hardened well ordered band of men. Even those, such as Hassan, who were not Scots born, had become a part of the fighting group. When a brigand corsair tried to board us in the Mediterranean Sea he received a good deal more than he bargained for, and was driven off with a shower of well aimed arrows, each one taking a toll of the pirates.

We encountered the tail end of a storm somewhere south of Sicily and found a shepherd lad floating helplessly far off the coast in a tiny coracle. He explained in sign language that he had been swept to sea by a storm, and was duly grateful for being rescued, expressing himself willing to accompany us wherever we might be going. We named him 'the Roman', for we thought, wrongly as it later transpired, that he was from that country. It turned out that in truth he was from Greece, and he proved to be a master with the pipes. His sons also inherited his pipe playing skills.

(*His sons were, of course, the MacRomans who became the hereditary pipers to the Chiefs of Gleneil down the centuries. They all seem to have had a somewhat roving Mediterranean eye and temperament and it is claimed, although on somewhat dubious authority, that it was a by-blow who sired the famous line of pipers on Skye, the Macrimmons. The lyric MacRoman's Roses sung by The Gleneils may be heard on the LP Tape of the Sound of Gleneil, also on the C-D Rom of The Clan Gleneil, and makes clear the fickle roving temperament of the MacRomans.*)

We encountered another brigand corsair, better armed than the first, but again our fighting skills repelled him without loss on our side and we continued our voyage despite contrary winds . . . (*Here again there appears to be quite a large part of the manuscript missing. It simply ends abruptly at this point and continues when Gleneil and his company had returned to Edinburgh. It seems likely that, being well armed and a competent fighting force, they returned through France the way they had come without any great difficulty. Although returning Crusaders were supposedly given free right of passage those not in a position to enforce their rights often found themselves victimised and even imprisoned if they could not make a suitable payment to those whose land they were crossing. The classic example of such cynical contempt for international agreements was, of course, the treatment of the commander of the 3rd Crusade, Richard Yea and Nay himself,. Unfortunately such contempt for international agreements still seems widespread in many parts of the European Union.)*

On our triumphant return to the court at Edinburgh I was surprised to be greeted warmly by a young woman of considerable presence and beauty, whom at first I did not recognise. I could hardly believe for some time that this was my erstwhile favourite childhood companion, Ann, sister to my bosom friend and companion Alan Fraser. It was not long before our old easy friendship turned on both sides to a deep and abiding love. With the approval of her father the old Chief and the king my father we were wed in the Spring with the newly knighted Sir Alan Fraser at our nuptials.

With the help of many of the Clan Fraser and with our own well disciplined force from the Crusade we were not long in building the Castle in a favoured spot by the lochside in Gleneil. Despite its difficulty of access Gleneil was a favoured south facing site, well sheltered by the hills with good glens and moors above the fertile strath. It was also well watered by its loch and river providing ample fish for our needs, With the Boar long gone, but his reputation still well remembered, his successors had ranged the glens and the strath at will without anyone attempting to evict them. When my followers moved in they found the virgin soil well repaid their efforts to till it, and the cattle we brought with us soon waxed fat on the lush grasses. Since most of my men not already married had followed my example and taken wives to themselves we soon also had a growing population in the glen.

My father, the King, was, I fear, little pleased that I had no great interest in affairs of state and was content, as he saw it, to turn my back on the court and to withdraw to my own fiefdom. Truth to tell I found the backbiting and intrigue in court circles little to my taste. I made a point, however, of visiting the court at least once a year and taking my rightful place in any deliberations where it was suitable. He in turn graced us with his presence on his few visits to the north and so we remained on good terms.

Since my return to Scotland relations between myself and the Macdonnels had, understandably, been strained. Although in some ways they could have been considered our neighbours, being situated beyond the Frasers and in parts almost adjacent to Gleneil they were separated in fact by a range of rugged mountains and some miles of marshy ground containing a number of bottomless bogs in which it was possible to lose a horse or a man with ease. We saw little or nothing of them, and were content to leave it that way until time had helped them to forget their grievances, real or imagined.

I was delighted when my new wife Ann gave birth to twin sons, soon after we had moved into our Castle at Gleneil. They were baptised Iain and William and proved to be a strong pair of infants. At their birth we were surprised to see each bore a red birth mark on the back of their left hand exactly where the nail intended to crucify me had been thrust into my own hand. This was regarded then as a remarkable omen, but it has since appeared in all my male begetting, and has then been passed on to their sons in turn. It is known far and wide as the Mark of Gleneil.

The boys' wet nurse was supervised by my old saviour, Jeannie Macdonald, who had insisted on coming with us to Gleneil along with Alistair Macgruer, whom she had married. I am not sure if he would have left his beloved Beaulieu otherwise, but she insisted on joining me and he had little choice in the matter but accompany her. I, of course, was pleased to have him, just as Fraser was loath to lose him, but Jeannie was a powerful character as will have been gathered and over-rode all their objections.

We were a small enough clan, but the surroundings were fair and made for a healthy life. Our youngsters flourished and life seemed good and so another year passed. When the time came for me to go south to the court to meet my father I left Gleneil with regret, but confident that in but a month or two I would return to find all well and Ann, who was with child again, perhaps with another son to join his brothers. There seemed not a cloud on the horizon to spoil our peace.

It was a fortnight or so later that I arrived in Edinburgh and almost at once I was greeted by Alan now Chief of the Clan Fraser following the death of his father the previous year. Alan's face was grim as he hastened forward to meet me.

"I have bad news," he said. "It seems James Macdonnel was not killed as we thought. He is alive and recovered, back in Scotland and swearing vengeance on you."

"Where did you hear this and from whom?" I demanded. "And do you believe it to be true?"

"I fear it is true enough," he answered. "My cousin Duncan, who was with us in Acre, saw him in Inverness. That was a month back, and he had just returned with a great scar across his face. Duncan said he would not have known him, for the slash you gave him has twisted his mouth and nose beyond recognition, but he was sure it was him once he spoke to him."

"Why has it taken so long for him to return?" I demanded.

"It seems after your combat his own clansmen thought he was dead, and his body was handed over to a Saracen wise woman to sponge down and prepare for burial," explained Alan. "She it was who found signs of life still in him and tended him with her own herbal unguents, oils and potions which appear to have gradually effected a cure. It seems, however, that it took a full two years in the Holy Land for him to recover sufficient strength to consider facing the return to Scotland. Since then it appears he and the one faithful clansman who stayed with him had a somewhat lengthy journey on their return overland which took them a further two years."

"And you say he is vowing vengeance?" I said thoughtfully. "That sounds like him, especially if his face is badly scarred. He was always vain of his looks. It is a pity I did not make sure of him on the field. It seems our lives are bound together and our destinies intertwined by fate."

"What will you do about it?" asked Alan.

"I must see the King, my father, and tell him that I am returning home at once," I replied. "My place is with my wife and sons if James is back in this country and wishes to do me a mischief, for he was never one to miss the chance of attacking where he thought the most damage could be done."

For a fleeting instant I could have sworn I smelt the scent of fresh cedarwood and felt the Nubian guards holding my wrists as I stood before the cross. It was a haunting memory that would always stay with me of the moment when I had almost resigned myself to death, and I knew now that I had James Macdonnel to thank for it. I had not appreciated the depth of his hatred then, but now I felt a sudden chill of fear at the thought of my wife and family at home in Gleneil and unaware of their danger.

"Yes," I repeated. "I must see the King, my father, at once. I must return home immediately. And thank you, Alan, for giving me this news."

In truth my mind was in a turmoil. It seemed almost impossible that he could be alive when I thought of the blood gushing through the visor of his helm and the effort I had had to make to disengage my blade so deeply was it sunk into the metal. At the time there had been no sign of life, and I had been sure then that he was dead. It was hard to believe that he was not only alive but back in Scotland and nearer my wife and sons than I was myself. That he was swearing vengeance I could readily believe. He had been filled with hatred before, for no really good reason beyond his own misguided envy, but how warped his mind must be now I almost shuddered to think. The man hated me and anything connected with me. The sooner I could return to Gleneil to protect my family the better.

I hastened to find the King, my father, brushing aside some flustered courtiers who tried to bar my access to his private bed-chamber. Thusting open the door unceremoniously I found him only half dressed on a couch with a naked wench beside him.

"What do you think . . ." he began angrily, but I was in no mood for niceties and interrupted him before he could say more.

"James Macdonnel was not killed in the Holy Land," I said. "He is alive and has been seen within the month in Inverness. He has sworn to revenge himself on me and mine, and I must return at once to Gleneil."

Even in such circumstances the King, my father, was a man of considerable regal dignity. As I turned to go he raised a hand to detain me. Then, rising to his feet, he covered the girl with a coverlet and thrust his arms into a gown.

"If he makes any move to harm you or any of your kin we declare him outwith the law," he declared. "And you may deal with him as you will."

He took a pace towards me and gave me a rare embrace.

"Now go and good fortune go with you," he said, clapping me on the shoulder as I turned towards the door.

I left Edinburgh with Alan, who insisted on accompanying me, and with a small company of our clansmen was in time to catch the wind and tide at Leith on a vessel just setting out for Inverness. The captain had intended making a series of calls at various ports on the way, but was soon persuaded that it would repay him well to make as swift a voyage as he could. Even so I fretted with impatience as contrary winds forced us to sail far out to sea in order to make headway north. In the end it was a full week before we made port, and I have never been so pleased to see the snow capped mountains beyond Inverness gleaming white and sparkling in the afternoon light.

I was in a fury of impatience as we rowed into the harbour and was not long in hiring horses to speed us on our way to Gleneil. Followed by the bulk of our companions on foot, Alan and I set as good a pace as the horses could muster, Even so it was getting dark as we at last sighted the pass of Gleneil. In my impatience I spurred my flagging beast to a final effort, Then at the mouth of the pass I leaped down and cast the reins of the exhausted beast aside, for I knew that in the confines of that rocky narrow and twisting ravine I would make better speed on foot.

I was soon well ahead of Alan, who was however following me at a good pace. Then I reached the final turning and saw Gleneil castle at the edge of the loch in front of me. There was a pall of smoke in the air above the battlements and I could see a mass of men fighting around the castle. More to the point and nearer at hand, I could see two bodies lying by the lochside. Even from a distance, I recognised

Ann's favourite gown. The anxiety I had been feeling was suddenly submerged in a blinding anger and I do not easily recall anything much of the next few minutes beyond a feeling of seeing everything through a red mist and the murderous rage which seized me.

I was carrying a battle axe and had a targe on my left arm, and I am told that I was heard shouting the Gleneil war cry 'Cross me who dares' from the entrance to the pass, a full half mile away. I stopped briefly as I reached the bodies. Ann was lying on her back seemingly unmarked with her eyes wide open and her old familiar half mocking smile still on her lips. The back of her head strangely cushioned on a tussock of grass was crushed and bloody. Beside her my faithful companion and follower, John Weir, was lying dead with several wounds. His skull too was crushed, the mark of the morning-star, James Macdonnel's favourite weapon. I felt hot tears of rage and anguish coursing down my cheeks and briefly blinding me; then suddenly my murderous rage vanished. It was replaced instead by an ice cold determination to deal finally with the man who had done this, and a feeling of utter certainty that nothing on earth could stop me doing so. As I ran forward to the castle entrance I know that men shrank from me and two who were bold or rash enough to stand in my path had their skulls split open like ripe melons so that none others dared follow suit. I doubt if all Saladin's forces could have stopped my headlong rush at that moment.

Inside the entrance door I stopped short. The long banqueting table, which had been carved from one the great old oaks by the lochside only a year or so before and which ran nearly the full length of the hall, had clearly been used as a barricade to hold back the raiding party. It had been thrust back into the large open fireplace where the end in the fire was blazing furiously, and the hall was filled with clouds of smoke as it burned unchecked. There were all the signs of a spirited defence in the hall itself, for there were dead and wounded, some of whom I recognised as clansmen, lying on each side of the table .

Then, through the billowing smoke I saw James Macdonnel at the foot of the stairs. I barely recognised him at first. He was no longer the old debonair and handsome figure. Under the same locks of red hair his was now a hideously scarred and bearded face. The sword slash had missed his eye but the cheekbone was deeply sunken and the mouth twisted grotesquely so that his teeth were bared in a permanent snarl beneath a nose of which only the nostrils like twin holes remained. For some reason the beard had only grown patchily and the effect was bestial in every respect like the face of a wild boar in human form. As he stared across the entrance hall with his eyes glaring triumphantly at me I felt I was seeing the real man for the first time.

"Ha, the Bastard himself," he grunted, for, quite apart from his appearance, even his speech seemed greatly affected. "I have killed your wife and your devil's spawn and now have at you."

He charged across the room whirling the two handed sword with which he was armed. I countered with my battle axe and felt the heavy jar as the sword edge struck the shaft and the head of the axe flew off with the impetus of my blow. For a moment the two of us were unbalanced. I fell forward on one knee and he was carried across the room. When we turned our positions were more or less reversed with him now standing in the doorway and I with my back to the open fire. He charged forward eagerly at once with his sword going back for an overhead killing stroke. I turned on the instant and siezing a burning log from the fire, regardless of the flames, hurled it into his face with all my force. It hit him fairly in the centre of that grotesquely scarred face and he gave a muffled yell of pain. Stumbling backwards he dropped his sword and put both hands to his eyes.

By this time I was on him, and I gave him no chance to recover. The memory of one of the old wrestling tricks Jamie Douglas had taught me came easily to mind. I seized his arms and fell backwards curling my knees up to my chest and placing my feet in his stomach as we fell together then releasing them in a powerful double kick which sent him flying through the air across the hall. As luck would have it he landed in a tangle of limbs on the end of the table and slid head first straight into the blazing fire. There was a long drawn out animal-like howl of agony, and from then on everything seemed to happen as in a dream.

I remember rising to my feet and picking up his sword. Then it seemed suddenly as if all that ensued had been fated. It was a dreadful figure, hair and clothes aflame from head to foot, that staggered from the fireplace a moment or two later. His eyes gleamed madly still and he had his dirk drawn. Yet somehow he seemed to me more like a sick animal to be put out of its misery than a mortal foe who had slain my wife and unborn son. I swung his sword in what I felt certain in advance was a powerful killing stroke and saw it connect with the side of his neck. The blade was sharp and there was little resistance as it cut cleanly through muscle and bone. I watched almost with detachment as his head flew off his shoulders and his corpse slumped sideways in a writhing mass on the castle floor with a fountain of blood spouting from the great artery of his neck. For what seemed a long time I leaned on the bloody sword looking down in a daze at the still smouldering corpse.

"Well," Alan said at my shoulder, bringing me back to reality. "That has finally put an end to that. At least this time no Saracen witch will bring him back from the dead."

"No, but he has killed Ann, your sister and my wife," I pointed out bitterly. "And apart from John Weir I have yet to find out who else is dead."

"The men he brought with him are dead or fled," said Alan. "And you might have known that your people would fight hard. Ann sent Hassan back to warn your old protector Jeannie and her husband Alistair to go off into the heather with your sons when she saw them coming. She herself rallied the men at arms and ordered them to stand by while she went out with John Weir to try to parley with them, eight months gone though she was. She scorned him to his face and he hit her with the morning-star as she turned her back on him, despite John Weir's efforts to protect her."

There was a note of pride in Alan's voice and I found myself infected by it. Ann it seemed had not died in vain. Thanks to her efforts and to my redoubtable old nurse and protector Jeannie, it appeared our twin sons were alive and safe. I too felt a surge of pride at the thought, and I turned to Alan and clasped his hand warmly.

"Thank you, old friend," I said. "No-one could have done more than you. Let us now find out what the damage has been."

We strode out into the evening light, and our followers raised a cheer at the sight of us both, bloodied and smoke smeared as we were, for Alan had had his share of the fighting protecting my back from attack as he had often enough done before in battle. Prominent amongst those present I was particularly pleased to see Alistair's familiar lean figure accompanying his wife, my old nurse and faithful protector Jeannie. In her arms she held my twin sons safely wrapped in the shawl she had snatched up as she fled the castle. The infants were still sleeping peacefully unaware of the uproar or of the loss of their mother.

"I'd have stayed," Jeannie assured me anxiously. "But Ann sent orders through Hassan for me to take the twins away with Alistair. She thought she would be able to hold them off, but she wanted them safe."

"It's all right, Jeannie," I assured her. "You saved these two, which is what she wanted and you did the right thing, If they had been around they'd have been killed for sure. That's what he came for, to have his revenge on me. I'm just grieved I didn't get back in time. If I had Ann would still be alive."

"You canna blame yersel' for that," she answered. "And Ann wouldn't want you to either. She stood before him fair and square, but the man was aye wanting in his wits and he was far gone today. He was like a wild beast come out of his lair. He was set on killing anyone got in his way."

"Well, he met a fitting end this day like the Great Boar before him," observed Alistair warmly. "The Gleneils have a war cry that suits them well. It is good to see you back, sire, and these your sons will live to hunt and fight like their father yet."

I looked at my two infants, swaddled in their shawl, and suddenly the loss of Ann overcame me. She had been my childhood companion and a part of my life so long that it had seemed natural enough to take her as my wife on my return. During that halcyon Spring of our early marriage I had grown from a youth back from the wars into full manhood, and she in turn had blossomed from a maiden into full womanhood. In our three years together we had loved each other long and well and grown to be a part of each other.

The sense of loss pierced me deeply and I felt my throat convulse. I waved my companions all away, and sought a quiet spot by the lochside where the sobs wracked me and I wept like a child as I felt at last the full loss and sorrow of her death.

It was not long before darkness began to fall, but it was pitch dark and the stars were bright in the sky before I returned to the Castle to find something like normality had begun to return to the scene. The hall had been cleared of bodies, the wounded tended to and the great table, badly charred at one end, was returned to its rightful position. My lady Ann was laid out in our bedchamber and seemed as if but asleep. Even so I could hardly bear to look on her, but gave Jeannie directions that she should be buried by the lochside, where she had liked to sit of an evening. (*The mound still known as Lady Ann's grave was a favourite spot for the 19th-century Gleneil ladies to sit and sketch by the lochside, and is mentioned in the writings of many of them, particularly Alexandra Gleneil, the noted suffragette.*)

James's younger brother Donald, one of the wounded Macdonnel clansmen who had been captured, confessed that on his return from the Holy Land James had inspired fear rather than support from most of his clan, save for a few devoted followers. He swore that he himself had no wish to harm us personally, and with this assurance we let him and the others go in peace, for I had no desire to perpetuate a blood feud. James's body and those of his clansmen who had died in the attack were taken to the hill and left to be retrieved by those of their fellows who cared to return for them. The following morning they were gone.

The next day with a grieving heart I buried Ann and John Weir along with four other clansmen who had been killed in the fight. Afterwards I found myself sick of mind and unable to rest. For the moment Gleneil did not have the old power to please me. Normally I could find solace on the mountainsides, the moors, the strath or the glens. It was a place I loved to roam, but now I had an urge to get far away.

"Alan, my old friend," I said to him. "May I spend the night with you at Beaulieu? I must return to the court and tell my father what has happened here, and I have no wish for once to remain in Gleneil."

Alan looked at me with sympathetic understanding, and simply turned towards the door, shouting for a clansman to fetch the horses. Within a short time we were mounted and on our way down the winding pass of Gleneil. I was accompanied only by the lad, Hassan, but Alan rode with me and his clansmen followed on foot. I was filled with an abiding sense of guilt at having left Ann by herself in Gleneil at that time, but Alan wisely kept me talking of all that we had planned together for the years ahead. That evening back in the old familiar surroundings of Beaulieu perhaps already my deep sense of loss was beginning to ease slightly as Alan and I discussed how to fulfil the plans Ann and I had made for the future.

The following day a gale was blowing from the west, and such a storm blew up that there was no prospect of taking a ship anywhere. The storm lasted for three days and nights and did much damage to buildings and trees. The wind howled like a pack of wolves all day and all night, and grown men were hard put to stand upright against the force of it. With it came hailstones the size of pullets' eggs, the like of which had never been seen in living memory. Then, on the fourth day, the sun shone and the wind turned to a gentle breeze from the east.

By then I was feverishly impatient to be on my way, and I was soon down at the harbour in search of a ship to take me, along with Hassan, on to Edinburgh. There was a scene of considerable devastation there. Several ships had it appeared been sunk by giant waves in the normally well sheltered moorings. Those ship captains whose vessels were still intact were reluctant to leave harbour. They all seemed convinced that the weather had not really abated, but that soon the storm would start again, and the older amongst them spoke gloomily of an even greater storm soon to come.

Although I offered them five good gold pieces to set sail as soon as was possible I met at first with a dour refusal from them all. Finally, however, avarice clearly got the better of one young sea captain, a fresh faced individual with an honest look about him. He came forward reluctantly, but spoke up fairly enough.

"I will take you, sire," he said. "There is another storm coming for sure, as we all know. But I have a wife and family and I need the gold.

I am in debt to the shipbuilder, who is my brother-in-law, and unless I pay him I will lose my ship anyway."

This was not the most reassuring of reasons for making the voyage, but it seemed to be my only choice, so I handed over the gold and took myself on board the small single masted carvel built barque. He was as good as his word and we were soon sailing seawards down the Firth. It was only when we reached the open sea that I noticed the big oily waves over which the boat climbed and swooped like a small piece of flotsam. We had barely altered course for the south when the wind started to howl in the rigging. The captain and his men made fast the sail, furling it tight against the mast, but even so we continued to sail before the wind almost as fast as before. The captain and his men threw a line overboard attached to a length of canvas and wood which had the effect of holding our head to the seas.

"We are heading for Norway now, but the sea anchor will stop us broaching to" he shouted. "There is no way we can make Scotland until this blows itself out."

In truth it was a humbling experience as the waves increased in size and the wind tore at the rigging. Hassan, never a good sailor, was soon lying below in a stupor of seasickness. Soon we were barely making the top of each mountainous wave, crawling slowly up the one side and hurtling down the other with a monotonous belly jerking motion. The wind rose to a scream, and in the great gulf between each giant wave it seemed our tiny vessel could never climb safely to the top and safely down the the side once more. More than one of the crew lashed to their various stations were mumbling prayers, and I could not blame them. So the hours passed, with every moment seeming likely to be our last. Darkness brought a further dimension of terror as every now and then a streak of lightning revealed our miserable state.

At some point during the hours of darkness the sail came briefly unfurled and was snatched away from the mast like a dish clout, disappearing in an instant with a sound like a clap of thunder which was barely audible above the roaring of the storm. Quite how the mast itself stayed intact, short and stubby though it was, it was hard to say. The ship's movements felt increasingly heavier and slower as she gradually filled with water. I felt sure we must soon be overwhelmed, but all we could do was try to bale out the water as each wave added to the weight on board. Then gradually the first streaks of dawn lightened the sky and slowly revealed our drawn and haggard faces and our wretched soaking wet condition.

Eventually, as the light increased, there came a point when almost imperceptibly the wind ceased to howl so strongly. Then the waves visibly began to decrease in size. By this time we were wallowing in the swells, barely able to stay afloat, but signs of the storm ending gave us fresh strength. The chain of leathern buckets, each filled and slopping over, moved towards the bulwarks and back with increasing speed, and slowly we began to see some effect. Soaking wet and freezing as we all were, the realisation that we might not drown after all was a most potent spur to action. Even Hassan, pale and wan, was eager to help.

"You'd not coax me into coming out again in weather like that no matter much gold you offer, or however deep I am in debt," remarked the young captain, in heartfelt tones. "How we remained afloat is more than I can tell."

For all his youth, he proved a competent seaman and an able captain for he soon had his men back at work, driving them on with oaths and by his own example. With some spare canvas stowed below deck for the purpose he rigged up a makeshift sail, and soon had us making headway before the now much reduced wind. Some herring, which might at one time have been dried, was produced and handed round. Though soaked with salt water it proved better than nothing, difficult as it was to chew. In addition there was a handful each of nearly dry oatmeal washed down with some water from a barrel lashed below decks which tasted old and sour. It was poor fare at best, but it was surprising how good it tasted and it seemed to put new life into us all.

Wet, cold and miserable though we were, we had good cause to be thankful for our survival. It was not long either before we came on unmistakeable traces of a shipwreck. Pieces of wood and lengths of cordage, oars and other flotsam were visible on the surface and with a long hook the crew did their best to rescue as much as they could. One or two bodies floating face down were also seen. Then one of the crew shouted excitedly.

"Straight ahead, someone still alive!"

There ahead of us on what seemed the mast and tattered remains of the sail of the wreck we could see an arm rise and fall, We closed on the mass of floating debris and saw two bodies lashed to the mast, both of whom seemed close to death. The one who had raised his arm was a yellow-haired fork-bearded young man of great stature, full six feet five inches with shoulders to match, who even in such dire straits managed to raise himself upwards. I unsheathed a dagger at my waist and leaned over to cut him free. As I reached down to slash the rope that bound him he glared at me with intensely blue eyes and waved me towards his companion. His meaning was plain and I reached beyond him to cut the lashing holding the smaller figure bound to the same spar.

The rope was easily enough cut but I nearly lost my hold on the water logged clothing as a wave splashed over us both. Then I had a firm grip and realised I had hold of a girl, or young woman, with such a strong facial resemblance to the man that they could only be brother and sister. With a strong heave I had her on board and as I laid her on the deck I saw her breasts rise and fall as she threw up several pints of salt water. I turned then and reached down to slash the rope that held the young giant. It required all my strength and the aid of a member of the crew before we could drag him on board. He too then spewed out what seemed like a good hogshead of salt water.

Looked at more closely, it was soon apparent that these were people of some consequence. Both were soaking wet, and had clearly been in the water for some time, each in the last stages of exhaustion. The girl, for she was only just past the threshold of womanhood, was dressed in a costly gown of silver cloth and the man wore a light tunic and hose of tanned skin with silver buckles of an intricate design. Although alive there was little more that could be said for them at that stage. I could scarcely have guessed then that this girl was to become my second wife and a worthy successor to my beloved Ann.

(Here to all intents and purposes the manuscript ends and only a few further fragments were readable, but it is evident from various points made that these two were the son and daughter of King Hakon of Norway. Subsequently the Princess Helga became Gleneil's second wife and outlived him. King William the Lyon died in 1214 but Iain Gleneil lived on until 1260. He ended his days according to legend with thirty six descendants each bearing the famed Mark of Gleneil all present at his death bed and with the Clan Gleneil well established.)

Editorial Footnote

The Editorial team is currently engaged in the very much less demanding task of editing the highly entertaining and extremely revealing diaries of the 18th Gleneil of Gleneil, Sir James Angus Neil of Gleneil, the younger twin brother of the 17th Gleneil of Gleneil. James was a reluctant Jacobite agent during the 1745 Rebellion, having been brought up on the continent by his uncle Calum Mohr Gleneil, a man of outstanding size, presence and physique and one of the leading exiled supporters of Charles Edward Stuart. At one time or another he met all the leaders of the various factions involved from Prince Charles Edward himself, and his advisors, Lord George Murray and the appalling John Wlliam O'Sullivan, to the leaders of the Hanoverian forces, including the almost equally appalling 'Butcher' Cumberland and the rather maligned General John Cope. Considering his remarkable insider's viewpoint, for at one time or another in his astonishing career he found himself talking to them all on equal, if not intimate, terms, his comments on both the Stuarts and the House of Hanover are extraordinarily interesting, providing some entirely fresh angles on the entire campaign. It also so happened that the Chief of the Clan Macdonnel of the day was known in Whitehall circles as 'Q' and was the leading government agent, while posing, naturally enough, as strongly pro-Jacobite. The strong antipathy between the chiefs of the two Clans, which had continued over the centuries since before the Third Crusade was finally to all intents and purposes ended by their bloody and drawn out confrontation during the 1745 Rising.

Those who have not so far encountered the Gleneils may wish to buy '*The Clan Gleneil,*' which contains the annotated history of the Clan Chiefs and 'A Review of the Clan Characteristics, Their

Background and the Land itself, Its Economic and Natural History, with a Look at their Garb and Way of Life in the Highlands, also their Close Connections with the Borders and Lowlands and Elsewhere Around the World, Including an Account of the Loch Gleneil Monster.' This gives the authentic background to the series of Clan diaries now being printed by the Gleneil Press. With each copy of the Clan history comes a handsome parchment certificate of Clan membership. This entitles the holder to wear the Ancient Clan Gleneil tartan, certified by the Tartan Society, and also to buy the Clan Gleneil malt whisky. Also recommended is the LP Tape of the Sound of Gleneil, by the Gleneils. (RRP £5) An entertaining Clan Gleneil C-D Rom is also available.(Tel: 01369 704144 for details) Membership of the Clan, it should be noted, also gives members the right to 20% reduction on all books bought direct from the Gleneil Press. P & P free within the UK only. Of particular interest to anyone interested in the Highlands is *The Scottish Highlanders & Their Regiments*: £14.99: ('This enjoyable book. Tom Pocock: *The Spectator*' 'Recommended reading to anyone.' Allan Douglas: *Edinburgh Evening News*:) Also strongly recommended is *Lady Evelyn's Cook Book* £12.99 by Evelyn Brander. ('How inspiring to find a cookbook so refreshingly different . . . Lady Evelyn's reminiscences bring laughter, even hilarity, to the text,.' *Scottish Homes & Gardens*) Together with *The Original Guide to Scotch Whisky*: (Paperback £4.99) by her husband, Michael Brander, these make a comprehensive guide to Scotland's basic food and drink.

For further details write to: The Clan Secretary, PO Box 13253, Haddington, EH41 4YA.

LOCHCARRON
of Scotland

Sole suppliers of The Ancient Gleneil Tartan

Visit our Mill at Galashiels and see the cloth actually being woven. Parties are shown round the mill regularly throughout the day. We make the finest tweeds and all the Clan tartans. Buy them and the best Scottish knitwear in our mill shop. Kilts, skirts, in tartan and tweed, stoles, the 'auld clan' tie and all the accessories for highland wear are available here. Make the most of your visit to Scotland by calling in to see us!

LOCHCARRON
of Scotland
The sign of quality

Lochcarron of Scotland
Waverley Mill
Galashiels
Scotland TD1 3AY

Tel 01896 751100
Fax 01896 758833

William E. Scott & Sons
Sporrans Edinburgh

Sole makers of The Clan Gleneil Sporran

William E. Scott & Sons (Sporrans), Edinburgh

Makers of Sporrans, Belts and Highland accoutrements to the Clan Gleneil and to the Trade around the world for four generations.

We make and design over 150 varieties of sporran. Send for our fully illustrated brochure.

Tel 0131 667 2506
Fax 0131 662 0529

William E. Scott & Sons (Sporrans)
112 Causewayside
Edinburgh, EH9 1PU
Scotland

Seven Towns Ltd.

7 LAMBTON PLACE
LONDON W11 2SH

The Kremers have been part of the Clan Gleneil since 1600. (See p.77 of 'The Clan Gleneil' history!) We have used our expertise and know-how to make money from ideas for toys and games. We have launched over 350 original toys and games in the past two decades alone, including Rubik's Cube and many others.

We now look to the Imagination and Creative Abilities of Clan members around the world

If you have any ideas for toys or games send them to us at Seven Towns. We may be able to turn them into reality on a royalty sharing basis.

MacRubik where are you?

Call David Kremer:

Tel 0171 727 5666
Fax 0171 221 0363

THE GUINEA GROUP

25 AINSLIE PLACE

EDINBURGH EH3 6AJ

Property developers like us, we feel,
Missed out on the chance to develop Gleneil

But from Gleneil country in the north we have
moved southwards to Loch Lomond in the west
and Kinross in the east where we aim to establish
another of our factory outlet villages. We have one
even further south in Essex at Clacton-on-Sea
where we provide a new experience in shopping.

Like the Gleneils before us we are also moving into
Ireland

Like all the Gleneils we do get around
Visit our villages where bargains abound

THE GUINEA GROUP

25 AINSLIE PLACE

EDINBURGH EH3 6AJ

TEL 0131 220 6535

FAX 0131 225 2330

CLASSIC CASTLES

BY

CANTOS ARCHITECTS

WE HAVE BEEN PROUD TO ADVISE
THE GLENEILS WHERE TO PUT IT
OVER SEVERAL GENERATIONS

"MORE MOAT FOR YOUR GROAT"

TEL 0171 388 7337
FAX 0171 388 7338

e-mail cantos@pipex.dial.com